WELCOME TO MY NIGHTMARE

There were six corpses arranged bizarrely around the cabin. All had been stripped naked. All were rotted beyond recognition, their bones exposed in spots, ribbons of flesh hanging from their bodies. Two were seated on the settee, one was sprawled on the top of the dinette table, and two lay on the floor, their arms neatly aligned at their sides, their grisly, ragged lips pulled back to expose their yellowing teeth in ghastly grins of welcome.

"My God," Percy declared in horror.

*Other Thrilling Adventures
in the* **OMEGA SUB** *Series
from Avon Books*

(#1) OMEGA SUB
(#2) COMMAND DECISION
(#3) CITY OF FEAR
(#4) BLOOD TIDE

Coming Soon

(#6) RAVEN RISING

Avon Books are available at special quantity discounts for bulk purchases for sales promotions, premiums, fund raising or educational use. Special books, or book excerpts, can also be created to fit specific needs.

For details write or telephone the office of the Director of Special Markets, Avon Books, Dept. FP, 1350 Avenue of the Americas, New York, New York 10019, 1-800-238-0658.

DEATH DIVE

J.D. CAMERON

AVON BOOKS · NEW YORK

If you purchased this book without a cover, you should be aware that this book is stolen property. It was reported as "unsold and destroyed" to the publisher, and neither the author nor the publisher has received any payment for this "stripped book."

OMEGA SUB #5: DEATH DIVE is an original publication of Avon Books. This work has never before appeared in book form. This work is a novel. Any similarity to actual persons or events is purely coincidental.

AVON BOOKS
A division of
The Hearst Corporation
1350 Avenue of the Americas
New York, New York 10019

Copyright © 1992 by David Robbins
Published by arrangement with the author
Library of Congress Catalog Card Number: 91-92086
ISBN: 0-380-76492-X

All rights reserved, which includes the right to reproduce this book or portions thereof in any form whatsoever except as provided by the U.S. Copyright Law. For information address Siegel & Siegel, Ltd., P.O. Box 20304, Dag Hammarskjold Postal Center, New York, New York 10017.

First Avon Books Printing: January 1992

AVON TRADEMARK REG. U.S. PAT. OFF. AND IN OTHER COUNTRIES, MARCA REGISTRADA, HECHO EN U.S.A.

Printed in the U.S.A.

RA 10 9 8 7 6 5 4 3 2 1

Dedicated To:
Judy,
Joshua,
and
Shane.

Prologue

The pungent smell of burning flesh, carried by a stiff northwesterly breeze, wafted across the open water to the small island and prompted the pair of men who were standing on the narrow stretch of beach to cover their noses with their hands.

"They're at it again," commented the leaner of the duo, and coughed lightly. He wore a brown shirt and jeans, both torn in spots, and carried a Winchester in the crook of his right arm.

"Won't the bastards ever stop?" asked the other, a man whose curly black hair hadn't been combed in a month. Like his companion, he wore clothes that once would have been tossed into the trash without a second thought. Strapped around his stocky waist was an Arminius .357 Magnum.

"I doubt it, Sal," said the rifleman.

"It makes me sick to my stomach. Night after night of the same damn thing, with them burning everyone they can lay their hands on, alive or dead. If I had a nuclear bomb, I'd drop it on what's left of New York City and wipe out the whole bunch."

The rifleman glanced sharply at his friend. "You would, huh? Hasn't there been enough of that bullshit already?"

Sal did a double take, then nodded. "Yeah, I guess there has, Pete. Sorry. But those crazies get to me."

"They get to all of us," Pete said.

For a few minutes the two men said nothing. They

simply stood and watched the distant fires flicker and dance as if alive. The inky silhouettes of structures that had once been magnificent skyscrapers dominated the skyline, dully reflecting the pale light from the full moon.

"What time is it, anyway?" Sal inquired.

"Past eleven."

"Then I guess I should be turning in. Marge will be ticked off if I stay up too late. You know, even after all these months she still has nightmares about the war and wakes up whining and crying in the middle of the night."

Pete nodded and pursed his thin lips. "I wonder if any of us will ever really get over it. It's not like World War Three can be compared to a bad car accident or a plane crash. It takes more than just filing it in the back of our minds to cope."

"Ain't that the truth."

From across the bay came a shrill, wavering scream that went on and on until it abruptly ended.

"Oh, God," Pete said in disgust. "They found another survivor."

Clenching his fists in anger, Sal stalked to the water's edge and shouted in frustration, "Damn you! Damn you all to hell!"

"What good does that do?" Pete asked. "You know there isn't a thing we can do about it." He paused, then added forlornly, "We're stuck here until *Liberator* comes."

Sal spun around. "Do you really think they'll make it all the way from the South Pacific? That's a hell of a long way. Must be a couple of thousand miles."

"More like six or seven thousand."

"You're kidding."

"I wish I was. Anything can happen to them over that great a distance."

Again they fell silent, contemplating the hopelessness of their situation.

"Well, I'd better get inside," Sal remarked, and headed for the remains of the college building on the rise above them. The bottom windows in the clock tower were illuminated by lanterns within. Off to the right creaked their makeshift windmill, on the verge of breaking down. Once it did, they could forget about using their shortwave. "Are you coming?"

"I guess so," Pete said, and started to turn when he heard a faint noise. "Did you hear that?"

"Hear what?"

"I don't know. Sort of a splash."

"Give me a break, buddy," Sal said, grinning. "It was probably a fish. You must be edgy tonight."

"I suppose," Pete said, and hefted his rifle. He peered at the surface of the bay but noticed nothing unusual. Shrugging, he pivoted and took several strides, thinking of how lucky their families had been to survive Armageddon and wondering if they were foolish to hope there would be a future. If they hadn't made contact using the shortwave radio, their chances of long-term survival would have been practically nil. But they *had* reached someone, the one man in all the world who could help them, could save them from the hell-hole that had once been the glorious Big Apple.

What a waste, Pete reflected, yearning for the days not long ago when his biggest routine worry was dealing with rush hour traffic. The Statue of Liberty. Times Square. The Empire State Building. Saint Patrick's Cathedral. The Brooklyn Bridge. They were all gone now, reduced to radioactive dust or charred steel skeletons. Where once had existed the most famous skyscraper-filled skyline in the world there was now an eerie expanse of unparalleled destruction inhabited by bloodthirsty crazies.

How could they have gone and done it? Pete asked

himself for the thousandth time. How could the leaders of the world have let the nuclear buttons be pushed after so many decades of relative peace? Who started it? Why? Did it even matter anymore?

Another, louder, splash sounded in the bay.

Pete halted and turned, expecting to see concentric rings of water on the placid surface where a fish had dived after leaping into the air, but there were no rings, no fish. Instead, something moved to the west at the very limits of his vision. "Sal?" he said.

"What is it?"

"There's something out there heading this way."

Already twenty feet from the beach, Sal stopped and cast an anxious glance out over the expanse of water forming the enlarged Lower Bay. He barely made out a few of the smaller islands off to the east and west, none of which were inhabited. The surface was tranquil. "I don't see anything. Quit trying to be funny."

"I'm dead serious. Take a look for yourself."

Sal retraced his steps and stood next to his friend. A sudden intake of breath signified he'd spotted whatever it was out on the water.

"A small boat, you think?" Pete asked, straining to distinguish details. All he saw was a vague, low form coming steadily nearer.

"It's too little to be a boat," Sal replied. "Maybe it's a fish or a shark." He paused and said almost as a prayer, "*Please* let it be a fish or a shark."

"There's no fin that I can see. And it's not swimming like a fish would."

"Debris, then," Sal suggested. "Maybe it's some junk being carried out by the tide."

"Then what are those things moving at its sides?"

"How should I know?" Sal answered testily.

Neither man budged or spoke as the object came close enough to identify.

"It's a log!" Sal blurted.

"And there's somebody on it!" added Pete.

They hurried down to the water, each man tense with expectation.

"It must be a survivor," Sal declared happily. "Someone made it out of the city."

"Maybe they saw our lights and decided to take the risk," Pete mentioned, equally as elated. "No one has ever made it out here. We'll have to roll out the red carpet."

Sal leaned forward. "Wait a minute."

"What's the matter?"

"Is that person wearing *white*?"

A tingle of dread rippled down Pete's spine as he squinted and focused on their visitor's clothing. Sure enough, the person, a man evidently, wore a white shirt. "Oh, God!"

Sal gripped Pete's forearm. "What the hell do we do? It's one of them!"

"Calm down," Pete advised, getting a grip on his own emotions. "We don't know that yet. It could be a coincidence. After all, those things don't have the brains to do something like this. Sometimes I think they don't have brains, period."

Backing up a step, Sal nervously fingered his revolver. "I don't know, buddy. I've got a bad feeling about this."

So did Pete, but he wasn't willing to admit it, not yet, not until he was positive. "Let's not do anything hasty. If you're right, we have plenty of time to take appropriate action."

"Appropriate, my ass. If I'm right, we can't let that thing step onto the island and you know it."

Pete nodded and leveled the Winchester, a 30–30, then levered a round into the chamber just in case. If they were right, the implications were terrifying. The only reason they'd lasted as long as they had was because the bay served as an impassable barrier between the horrid white-shirts and the island. Until now, the zombies, as he preferred to call them, had never tried to cross the barrier. If one did, the rest were sure to follow suit eventually, which meant their island retreat was no longer a safe haven.

The thought almost made him laugh. Was there any place on the whole planet that qualified as a safe haven? The guy who commanded the nuclear sub thought so, but he could be wrong. Maybe trying to survive was useless. Maybe, sooner or later, the radiation would kill them all.

"Here he comes," Sal said breathlessly.

Now close enough for the man's face and arms to be seen clearly, the log and its passenger made directly for them.

"He sees us," Sal exclaimed.

"Yeah," Pete said, and the short hairs at the nape of his neck tingled when he distinguished the wicked grin creasing their visitor's face. "Damn! It is one."

"I knew it!" Sal bellowed. He drew the .357 and squeezed off two shots, holding the revolver in a two-handed grip to steady his aim.

The white-shirt's head jerked backwards and the body started convulsing wildly.

"Die!" Sal shouted, and fired again.

Suddenly the crazy went limp. The arms that had been stroking so regularly dropped into the water, but the log drifted nearer, propelled by its momentum.

"Stop it," Sal declared. He sent two more rounds into the white-shirt, the booming of the Magnum seeming to echo across the bay, but neither accomplished anything.

Pete cast about for a branch or a pole, for any object they could use to prevent the log from reaching the beach. To his dismay, nothing was handy. Acting on impulse, he ran into the water, gripped the Winchester's stock firmly, and extended the barrel.

"What are you doing?" Sal asked.

"What's it look like?" Pete retorted, bracing his legs. He disliked being so close to one of the things, afraid whatever caused their condition might be contagious. If he succumbed, what would happen to his wife and kids? Sal would have a hard time trying to provide for both families.

The huge log struck the end of the Winchester, the impact jarring Pete and forcing him to tuck his elbows against his sides to keep from being bowled over. A reeking odor assailed his nostrils, the bodily stench of someone who hadn't bathed in ages, and he felt bile rise in his throat.

Sal entered the water. "You did it," he stated happily.

"Give me a hand and we can shove this back out," Pete proposed. "The tide will take it from there."

"Gladly." Sal moved close, holstered the Arminius, and reached for the end of the log, then hesitated. The white-shirt's head was within inches of the edge, resting on its left cheek, a pale, pink fluid seeping from the bullet holes.

Pete sensed his friend's revulsion at being so close to the corpse, a feeling he shared. "Just grab the rifle," he suggested, and remembered it was ready to fire. "Be sure not to touch the trigger."

Nodding absently, his gaze riveted on the thing, Sal took hold of the Winchester. "Look at all the sores," he said softly.

Dozens of ugly sores dotted the white-shirt's face and hands, transforming what had once been a relatively handsome man into a grotesque travesty of humanity.

"Disgusting," Sal commented.

"Just push," Pete said. "On the count of three."

"Okay."

"One."

"I wish we could burn it," Sal remarked.

"Two."

"If I ever turn into one of those things, promise me you'll blow my brains out."

Pete ignored him and finished the count. "Three." He started to shove, using the rifle as a prod, and the log glided backwards, but it only went a few inches when the crazy abruptly gasped, blinked, and sat up.

"No!" Sal declared, letting go and sweeping the revolver out. He squeezed the trigger and produced a loud click, nothing more. "Damn! I need to reload. Shoot it!"

Encouragement wasn't necessary. Pete sighted on the thing's forehead, held his breath, and fired. The recoil drove the stock into his shoulder, and the impact of the slug knocked the white-shirt onto its back. Pete fed another round in and took a bead again, pausing when he realized the crazy wasn't moving.

"One more time for good measure," Sal prompted.

"We can't afford to waste ammo, and you know it. I think it's finally dead."

"You *hope* it is."

They watched as the log drifted farther out.

"I've got an idea," Sal said.

"What?"

"The next time we go to the mainland, let's try to find some grenades."

"Dream on."

"There must be grenades somewhere. Maybe in an armory located outside of the blast radius."

Pete half expected the thing to sit up at any moment. He nervously licked his lips and listened to cries of alarm coming from the house.

"Hell, if we could locate an armory, we'd have all the guns and explosives we'd ever need," Sal continued.

8

"M16s. Mortars. Machine guns."

"Why not round up a tank while we're at it?"

"Now you're talking!"

Shaking his head, Pete relaxed as the log kept going. There were other priorities they needed to work on. First and foremost would be a barrier of some kind, a high fence perhaps, constructed either of wood or barbed wire if they could obtain enough, completely encircling the island. It would be a bear of a job, but at least they'd be able to sleep without fear of those things creeping up on them in the middle of the night.

"Do you figure we should tell Donovan?" Sal inquired.

"Why?"

"He might like to know."

"What purpose would it serve? He already knows our situation, and he promised to get here as fast as he can. There's nothing we can do but wait and pray *Liberator* arrives before the white-shirts attack us in force."

"Maybe he could give us advice on how to deal with them," Sal stubbornly persisted.

"Donovan doesn't know anything about them that we don't. He's already told us as much."

"Why are you being so pessimistic?"

An involuntary cackle erupted from Pete's lips.

"Pessimistic? Here we are, survivors of World War Three, stuck on an island in the middle of a bay that's overrun with sharks, with hordes of zombies lurking on the mainland and just waiting for the chance to feed us to their bonfires, barely managing to put enough food on the table for our wives and kids, and you ask me what the hell I have to be pessimistic about?"

It was a full five seconds before Sal responded. "I see your point. Guess I was being stupid."

A twinge of guilt at his sarcasm pricked Pete's conscience. "I'm sorry," he apologized.

"You have nothing to be sorry about. You're right. If Donovan doesn't get here soon, there won't be anyone to rescue."

1

Captain Thomas P. Donovan awoke slowly. He could feel the morning sunlight on his face and chest, warming his skin, and he grinned at the pleasant sensation. Vivid memories of the previous night, of the intimate embraces he'd shared with the woman he loved, filtered through his consciousness and widened his grin into a contented smile. Who would ever have thought that anyone could know such happiness after the world had gone and blown itself all to hell? The irony amused him. In a certain sense, he was more content now than he'd been before the war, and he could only attribute his newfound satisfaction with life to Alex.

Donovan opened his eyes and squinted out the open window at the coconut palm growing near their hut. Golden rays streamed inside, revealing him in all his naked glory, and cast a yellow glow over his softly slumbering companion. He glanced at her, at the rhythmic rising and falling of her breasts, and gave thanks for another day in Paradise.

Alexandra Fisher was as lovely in repose as she was awake. Dark hair cascaded well past her shoulders. High cheekbones and a narrow face gave her an elegant appearance belied by her forceful, practical personality. The daughter of an Episcopalian minister, she had a twin brother named Peter who was a skilled surgeon and medical researcher. Alex had specialized in computer science and possessed an encyclopedic knowledge of history and politics. At Donovan's urging, she'd agreed to serve as the science specialist on *Liberator*.

Imagine, he reflected. The only female crew member, and she cared exclusively for him. Sometimes, when the sub was on an extended cruise and a few of his men were grumbling about how much they missed their sweethearts and families, he'd feel a twinge of guilt at his good luck. Fortunately, as soon as the two of them were alone in his cabin, his guilt promptly evaporated. If someone had to have his cake and eat it too, why shouldn't it be him?

Donovan stretched and inhaled the cool, tangy air. Sea air could be so invigorating, and a westerly breeze was blowing in off the Pacific. The thought of the ocean brought to mind his ship, the reason he and all the other survivors were there on the South Pacific island of Espiritu.

The U.S.S. *Liberator* was a nuclear-powered Omega-class submarine, the ultimate in undersea technology constructed shortly before the outbreak of the ultimate insanity. At the moment the missiles were launched, *Liberator* had been under the North Pole on a test run. If not for the protective layer of ice overhead, she might have suffered the same fate as 99 percent of the oceangoing vessels in the world: instant obliteration.

Sitting up carefully so as not to disturb Alex, Donovan stared out the window at the micronuke that had been installed by *Liberator*'s chief engineer. Placed on a concrete platform to prevent shifting in case of a typhoon, the MicroScale Home Nuclear Unit was compact and built in modular fashion. The stacked components resembled an old-fashioned stereo system, and there were very few wires and tubes. A black box no bigger than a suitcase contained the thermopile, while another black module as large as a trunk housed the compact nuclear furnace. According to Chief Smith, the micronuke would supply all of the survivors' power needs for the next forty years.

Also visible were other huts—typical South Pacific affairs with circular walls and conical roofs. Interspersed among them were mango, breadfruit, and hibiscus trees, as well as the ubiquitous palms. The settlement itself was situated in the very center of Espiritu, spread out over a wide, flat area.

Donovan stood, found his underwear and pants lying on the floor, and put on both. He hitched at his belt as he padded from the bedroom into the living area. Like all the huts, this one left a lot to be desired in the way of accommodations. Since the natives had gotten by quite nicely without the use of furniture, and electricity had been nonexistent, the survivors were busily engaged in bringing the living standard up to Western par. Those who possessed carpentry skills and electronic know-how were hard-pressed to meet the demand for their services.

Several trips had already been made to Tahiti and other nearby islands to obtain necessities like power tools, refrigerators, and blow-dryers. The deserted towns contained all the supplies the survivors would ever need. One woman had even compared going on a supply run to "a free shopping spree."

Donovan didn't like taking things without paying for them, or at least asking the owners, but there were no owners to ask and money was now worthless. Dollar bills and leaves had become the substitutes of choice for toilet paper.

The one postwar aspect that bothered Donovan the most, though, was the absence of people in cities and communities that were virtually unscathed by the holocaust. On island after island where civilization once flourished and hordes of tourists once roamed, there were buildings and vehicles galore but no inhabitants. It was a spooky feeling to be walking down a deserted street past stores and homes in perfect condition, knowing there wasn't a living soul anywhere. Every time Donovan ventured into a town, he was reminded of the old "Twilight Zone" reruns on television. Only this was real.

He walked to the recently constructed kitchen on the south side of the hut and opened the compact refrigerator. A pitcher of orange juice, prepared by Alex last night from the last can of concentrate they'd owned, made him lick his lips in thirsty anticipation. He poured a glass and was replacing the pitcher when a pair of slim arms encircled him from behind and a husky voice whispered in his ear.

"Morning, sailor. Looking for a good time?"

Donovan chuckled and stroked her hands. "Good God, woman. Don't you ever get enough?"

"You've heard the phrase 'Light my fire'?"

"Yeah. So?"

"Just think of me as a towering inferno."

Laughing, Donovan turned and pecked Alex on the lips. Only then did he notice she was still in her birthday suit. "You shouldn't be traipsing around without any clothes on."

"Why not? It's our hut."

"Yeah, but what if one of the neighbors should see you?"

"They'll get the thrill of their lives."

"I'd prefer it if they get their thrills somewhere else," Donovan said, and playfully smacked her on the posterior. "Now go get dressed before you ruin my reputation."

Alex backed up and regarded him critically. "I had no idea you were such a prude."

"Blame my father and mother and my straitlaced middle-class upbringing. I was subjected to Sunday school, prayers at every meal, the whole works. Some of it must have rubbed off." Donovan motioned at the bedroom. "Now *please* get decent before my blood pressure goes through the roof."

"Remind me to sit down and have a long talk with you soon," Alex said over her shoulder as she walked off. "Your priorities are all screwed up."

Snickering at her unintentional pun, Donovan took his juice and stepped to a plain wooden rocking chair positioned near the large window in the east wall. One of these days, he mentally noted, he would have to put a glass pane in it to keep the bugs out.

"Say, did you happen to hear anything last night?" Alex called out from the bedroom.

"Just you moaning."

"I mean besides us, lover."

"Nope. Why?"

"I'm not sure, but I thought I heard a strange sound right before I drifted off. Sort of like a wailing noise."

Her comment caused Donovan to recall the weird nocturnal howling heard by all of the survivors at one time or another. No one knew what was responsible, and the hunting parties sent into the jungle were never able to find a clue. There were plenty of theories: wolves, unhinged islanders, even the wind whistling through the volcanic cone. If there were animals or natives lurking out there, they had plenty of space in which to hide.

Espiritu was ten miles long and four miles wide. Its shape resembled an enormous figure eight that had been laid on its side. Dominating the western half was the volcano, rearing two thousand feet above the ocean and silently spewing gray smoke into the atmosphere twenty-four hours a day. Encircling the base of the menacing cone was a lush jungle that extended in every direction except north, where a sheer cliff posed an impassable barrier. Some of the survivors had wondered aloud what might be on top of the precipice, but so far no one had let curiosity get the better of common sense and attempted to scale it.

In the middle of the island was the village, while the eastern end consisted of a circle of ancient volcanic rock and coral surrounding the caldera of an extinct sister to the brooding active volcano. Long ago the ocean had poured into the caldera, forming an apparently bottomless lake protected from sharks and other predators of the sea after the surrounding coral rose high enough to form a complete wall. An abundant variety of fish lived in the lake, providing an ample, nutritious food source.

The best beaches were on the south side and the northeast tip of Espiritu, and it was the latter broad strip of soft sand that attracted large numbers of survivors daily.

Donovan believed it possible there were animals that hid in the jungle during the day and prowled abroad at night, but not so much as a single track or clump of hair had been found. Posting sentries had proved fruitless; they all heard the howls, yet never saw the source.

"Did you hear me?" Alex asked, emerging dressed in jeans and a loose-fitting white shirt.

"I heard," Donovan responded, rousing from his contemplation. "I just wish we could get to the bottom of this before *Liberator* leaves for New York."

"When will that be?"

"Soon."

Alex stepped to the window, her back to him. "I seem to recall you said the same thing last week."

"And I'll keep on saying it until I'm certain it's safe for us to leave."

"You don't think the colonists from San Francisco can manage on their own?"

"It's not that," Donovan stated, wishing she would turn around so he could read her expression.

"Then what is it?"

"The colonists haven't been trained to handle combat situations."

Finally Alex rotated, and arched her eyebrows. "Sounds like the same thing to me, Tom."

"Hear me out," Donovan declared. "Let's suppose, for the sake of argument, that there's a pack of—something—roaming Espiritu. We don't know if these things pose a threat, but with so many women and children here we certainly don't want to find out the hard way. Sure, the colonists have firearms, but most of them couldn't hit the broad side of the volcano with a bazooka. Do you want me to just head on out to sea with this question mark hanging over all our heads?"

"We've been here almost two months. Surely if these animals are dangerous they would have attacked someone by now."

"Maybe they haven't had the right opportunity."

Alex shook her head. "Once a captain, always a captain."

"Meaning?"

"Meaning your life has been the Navy. You're accustomed to the responsibility of being an officer, to giving commands and being obeyed, to safeguarding the lives of others whether they want to be safeguarded or not. In short, to doing things your way. You've convinced yourself the colonists can't cut it, that they're lost without you to guide and protect them." Alex made for the kitchen. "You're wrong."

Donovan started to reply, then changed his mind. What if she was right? What if, deep down inside, he didn't want to relinquish any of the control he enjoyed as the ranking military officer on Espiritu? Old habits did die hard, and he had to admit he liked being in a position of authority. After all, he hadn't worked so hard at rising through the ranks to become the commander of a sub simply because he was fond of periscopes.

He knew he'd inherited his drive from his father, a highly decorated New York City police detective. The elder Donovan had been fiercely devoted to his job, a devotion attested to by a thick scrapbook filled with newspaper clippings of his major busts. The life of a cop meant long hours and other personal sacrifices, not the least of which was little time to spend at home. But when Detective Donovan was home, he'd invariably take his two boys down to his old wooden sailboat berthed at the Seventy-ninth Street Boat Basin in New York City.

That was where Donovan acquired his love of the sea. Many an idle hour had been spent in daydreaming of thrilling adventures in exotic ports of call. Donovan, at the age of fourteen, vowed to one day visit as many of those ports as he could, and his resolve served to fuel his entrance into the Navy.

My life in a nutshell, he reflected wryly, and finished off the orange juice. Standing, he took several strides toward Alex when the sound of rushing feet drew him up short.

A familiar face appeared at the front window. "Captain! Come quick! There's been an attack!"

Donovan was outside before the bearer of bad tidings could shout again and wake up everyone living within fifty yards of the hut. "What kind of attack, John?" he asked his second in command, intuitively fearing the worst.

Executive Officer John Percy pointed to the south, his rugged features animated by anger. He wore pants and a brown shirt, both rumpled, both evidently put on in haste. "The sentry is dead."

Alex materialized on Donovan's right. "Dead?" she repeated in disbelief.

"Afraid so," Percy responded. "Something jumped him on the perimeter of the village."

"What?" Alex asked.

"Take a look at the body, then you tell me," Percy said.

"Is anyone with the body now?" Donovan inquired.

"Yes, sir. The kid who found it. Bobby Hansen, one of the crowd from San Francisco. He was on his way to go fishing when he stumbled on the remains. Since my hut was closest, he came to get me first."

Donovan looked at Alex. "Do me a favor. Go tell your brother we need him. Then rouse my brother out of the sack and let him know I want a six-man detail, all well armed, at the spot within fifteen minutes."

"On my way," Alex said, and ran to the west.

Percy gestured impatiently. "I'll show you where it's at, Captain."

"Lead the way," Donovan said, and abruptly realized he still held the empty glass. "No. Wait a second." He dashed inside, put the glass down on the floor, then hastened into the bedroom and donned a white T-shirt and sneakers. In moments he was back out. "Now let's go."

The executive officer hurried southward. "Did you eat much of a breakfast?" he asked.

"Is it that bad?"

"You'll have to see for yourself."

Donovan scowled. His executive officer was a hard-as-nails firebrand who always went by the book. Percy always told the truth and nothing but the truth. He never exaggerated when making a report. If anything, he tended to understate the details. If the condition of the body had upset Percy so much, then Donovan knew he had to brace himself for the worst. Even so, he nearly lost the orange juice.

The guard lay on his back under a mango tree, his arms outspread, his blank eyes fixed on the limbs overhead. His head was untouched, as were his legs from the knees down. In between, though, the poor man's body constituted a mangled, ruptured mess of indistinguishable parts and pieces. Something had ripped him to ribbons, especially the abdomen and the thighs. Pulpy bits of intestines littered the ground. Already a putrid stench rose from the corpse.

Donovan thought of all the children who would soon be up and about, and glanced at Percy. "There's no need for everyone else to see this. Go get a blanket to cover him."

"Aye, Captain." The executive officer departed.

"Is there anything I can do, sir?" asked Bobby Hansen, a lean youth of fifteen or so who stood off to one side, his shock transparent.

"You can go home," Donovan advised.

"But I was thinking of going fishing."

"Not until we track down whatever did this."

Nodding, the teenager made off.

All alone, Donovan stared into the jungle and wondered if the animal responsible was out there at that moment, watching him. He wished he'd brought a firearm. A brightly plumed bird flew from a nearby tree, startling him, and he willed himself to calm down. Gazing at the dead man's face, he tried to recall the sentry's name. Webber, wasn't it? The guy used to be a plumber in San Francisco before the war. Thank God he wasn't married.

Squatting, Donovan scanned the ground for prints. He spotted a rifle lying under a bush and retrieved it. The hapless Webber hadn't managed to get off a single shot from the Rossi 44-40. Whatever jumped him had done so swiftly and silently.

The muted clank of dishes and pans, mingled with muffled conversations, came from the village. More and more colonists were greeting the new day.

Donovan walked in a circle around the corpse, examining every square inch of soil. There were flattened patches of grass, and at a circular barren spot the faintest impression of a large paw. Stunned by the discovery, Donovan lightly traced his fingers over the print. Distinct claw marks capped each of the four spherical toes, and there was a separate heel pad outlined quite nicely. He had no idea what type of track it might be, but at least he knew they were definitely dealing with an animal, not deranged natives, which in itself wasn't much consolation. Animals possessed heightened senses of hearing and smell. They would be harder to trace to their lair.

Percy returned bearing a green blanket. Without saying a word he draped it over the body, grimacing in revulsion.

"Thanks," Donovan said, standing.

"Did you find something?"

"Yeah. Take a look. Maybe you can tell me what we're up against."

But the executive officer could only shake his head in bewilderment after a minute spent inspecting the track. "Sorry, Captain. Beats me. I'm no Daniel Boone."

Together they examined more ground until Donovan saw Alex, his brother, and five crewmen approaching. "Didn't take you long," he commented.

"Pirate was already up," Alex explained, gazing at the blanket.

Pirate was the nickname of Donovan's younger brother, Charlie. The two had been inseparable as boys, and both eventually entered the Navy. Charlie, however, opted for a different career field. At the outset of the war he'd been a Technician First Class serving as a LAMP operator on a helicopter flying over the Bering Strait. After the chopper went down, he'd floated in a raft for days before being rescued by *Liberator*.

Unlike Donovan, Charlie possessed a passion for guns. He'd always been the better marksman, and distinguished himself by twice winning the Navy's pistol competition. In recognition of that expertise, Donovan had taken the liberty of appointing his brother First Gunnery Officer. When landing parties ventured ashore, Charlie invariably led them. He was fearless and headstrong, a combination that made him a tiger in combat.

The nickname Pirate stemmed from their childhood. Charlie had adopted it after viewing *Raiders of the Lost Ark* and spying the legend "Air Pirates" on the back of a pilot's shirt. Where Donovan had always been more interested in ships, Charlie enjoyed a fascination with planes.

"What have we got, Tom?" his kid brother now inquired.

"Take a look for yourself," Donovan replied. "Just don't inhale when you lift the blanket."

One by one, Charlie, Alex, and the detail all viewed the remains. A crewman abruptly covered his mouth and dashed into the trees, and everyone could hear his heaves.

Alex folded her arms and bowed her head. "Dear Lord," she said softly.

"Any clues?" Charlie asked.

"A print," Donovan disclosed, and indicated the spot so they all could study it.

"A cat of some kind, maybe?" Alex suggested.

"No," Charlie said. "Cats don't leave claw marks. I read it somewhere."

"One of the colonists used to hunt a lot," Percy mentioned. "Milsap, I think his name is. I know where he lives. Do you want me to go get him, Captain?"

Before Donovan could respond, Alex's brother, Dr. Peter Fisher, arrived. He wore shorts and had his hair tied in a ponytail. Clutched in his left hand was the black bag he'd taken to carrying on his daily rounds of colonists who needed medical attention. He'd yet to set up an office. In the interim, the sick bay on *Liberator* sufficed, but he only took those who were seriously ill aboard for tests and recuperation. Thankfully, except for two cases of food poisoning, most of his attention went to treating sore throats, sprains, and colds.

Dr. Fisher looked at the blanket and frowned. "Who was it?"

"Webber," Donovan said.

"Damn. I liked him."

"I need an autopsy right away. Anything you can tell me will be appreciated."

Kneeling by the deceased, Dr. Fisher examined the corpse for a minute, his expression clinically reserved.

"I don't think you need an autopsy to determine an animal is responsible."

"I want you to tell me what kind of animal."

"Even if I find hairs, blood, or saliva, our lab isn't equipped to make a comparison of every known species. We can match the basic types, but nothing exotic."

"Do your best."

Dr. Fisher replaced the blanket and stood. "I'll go to the ship and await the remains."

"Thanks, Pete," Donovan said, and turned to his executive officer. "You heard the man, Mr. Percy. Collect a detail and have the body taken on board. Afterward, bring Milsap here and let him examine the track."

"Right away, sir," Percy said, and hurried into the village.

"What will you be doing?" Alex asked.

Donovan nodded at the jungle. "We're going to go in after it."

"I'll tag along."

"I'd prefer for you to stay here," Donovan said. "Someone has to break the news to the colonists, and they all know and respect you. Call a general meeting to inform them of the attack. Keep them calmed down until I return. Under no circumstances is anyone to venture beyond the village, not even to pick fruit or to go sunbathing. Understood?"

"Yes, sir," Alex responded, accenting the last word.

Disregarding her sarcasm, Donovan looked at Charlie. "Are you all set?"

"What about provisions?"

"We'll only stay out until noon or so. If anyone feels like they're starving, there's plenty of food in the jungle."

"Then let's go slay a few dragons, big brother," Charlie said, grinning and hefting his submachine gun.

All of the men carried the Navy version of the compact Luigi Franchi 9-mm automatic. It sported a 32-round box-type magazine, an 8-inch barrel, and could fire 250 rounds per minute in the full auto mode. Once a favorite of revolutionary groups in Africa, Southeast Asia, and Latin America, the Franchi was constructed from rectangular welded tubing and could easily be repaired in the sub's machine shop.

"Stay alert," Donovan directed, and led them into the jungle.

"Take care," Alex called out.

Acting on a hunch, Donovan went in the direction indicated by the paw track, to the southeast. He skirted trees and clusters of dense brush, stepped over logs, and pushed trailing vines aside with the Rossi. Constantly searching the soil, he found nothing of significance until they had traveled over half a mile and came to a small spring. There, at the water's edge, was the evidence the colonists had long sought: dozens of freshly made tracks of all sizes. "At last," he said, and dropped to one knee.

"Look at all of them," Charlie declared. "There must be a whole pack."

Several of the crewmen glanced nervously at the wall of lush vegetation and fingered their Franchis.

"Whatever they are, we can't rest until we kill every one," Donovan stated. "If we don't wipe them out, no one will be able to go abroad at night. We'll have to construct a fence around the entire village to protect ourselves." He paused. "It'll be just like before the war, when we had the threat of a nuclear war always hanging over our heads. Only this time it will be the fear of being torn to shreds. I, for one, am tired of living in fear. We have a chance to make a secure future on Espiritu and I won't let anything stand in our way."

Charlie chuckled. "I had no idea you were this philosophical so early in the morning."

"Only when I don't get enough sleep."

"And what were you doing all night?"

"Insomnia," Donovan fibbed.

"Uh-huh."

Rising, Donovan motioned at the jungle. "Fan out," he ordered. "Try to find in which direction these things went."

Obediently, the crewmen spread around the spring and began a thorough sweep.

"Mind if I ask you a question?" Charlie commented.

"Be my guest," Donovan replied, watching the others.

"When are we leaving for New York City?"

"You too?"

"What?"

"Have you been talking to Alex?"

"Not about New York," Charlie said, studying his brother's face. "Why? What did she say?"

"She thinks I should get my butt in gear and head out."

"I agree. Those people on that island can't last forever. Do you realize we haven't heard a peep out of them in three days?"

"I know," Donovan said, thinking of the communications facility they'd established on the west side of the village. Thanks to a powerful transmitter set up by his chief engineer and an antenna the colonists erected high up on the eastern slope of the volcano, they possessed the capability to monitor broadcasts from around the globe. So far, though, such broadcasts had been few and far between. The airwaves were as dead as the majority of the human race.

A cause for celebration occurred when a shortwave transmission was received from two fishermen in New York, Sal Ronca and Pete Hardesty. Donovan had immediately set out to rescue them, but he ran into two problems when he attempted to get through the Panama Canal.

The first was in the person of a Panamanian dictator involved in a private war with drug lords from South America. Through circumstances Donovan couldn't control, he became embroiled in the conflict, delaying his attempt to reach the Atlantic Ocean.

But the second problem was the major one. During World War Three, one side or the other nuked the canal, transforming the 150-yard channel into a mile-wide waterway. The expansion created a raging funnel as the waters of the Pacific were drained into the Atlantic. At the east end of the canal a huge wall of sand hundreds of feet high and hundreds of yards thick had been created by a thermonuclear blast, and the cascading Pacific waters had poured over the rim with the thunderous force and din of a million Niagara Falls.

Liberator could never negotiate such a massive barrier. Donovan had opted to remove it using a Mark 97N tactical nuclear missile. After precise calculations were made and rechecked a dozen times, he put his plan into operation. Computer projections had shown that destroying the wall would create a powerful, unstable current in the canal, a current capable of severely damaging the sub. The computer also predicted erosion would widen the channel even more and stabilize the current sufficiently within a month to permit passage. So Donovan used the old hit-and-run technique, blowing the wall and running like hell out the west end before the full effects could be felt.

Now the month was up, plus two weeks extra, and Donovan knew he couldn't postpone the rescue mission much longer. He'd delayed in the hope of discovering the source of the howls. In a way, he wished he hadn't. How could he leave knowing there were man-eating animals on the island?

"Captain!" one of the men suddenly shouted. "Over here."

Donovan and Charlie were by the seaman's side in seconds, staring at a faint trail of tracks in the soft soil on the southwest side of the spring.

"Looks like they're heading toward the volcano, sir," the seaman noted.

"Yeah," Donovan drawled, wondering if the beasts had their lair in one of the many fissures marking the cone and the ground immediately below. He motioned for the rest of the detail to fall in.

"We should put someone on point," Charlie cautioned.

"Good idea," Donovan said, mentally chiding himself for not thinking of it first. Not that he expected a pack of animals to lay an ambush for them, but the old adage his mother had always used applied once again. Better Safe Than Sorry.

Charlie grinned and indicated a lean sailor. "Fitz, you're on point. Stay in sight and stay frosty."

"Yes, sir," the crewman replied, and headed out.

Donovan waited a suitable interval, then followed. His stomach growled, reminding him of the breakfast he'd failed to eat, and he wished he'd brought food along after all.

"You never did give me an answer," Charlie remarked.

"About New York?"

"No, the tooth fairy."

"We'll leave as soon as this situation is settled."

"And those poor guys waiting for us?"

"They can wait a while longer."

"Cold, brother. Very cold."

Donovan glanced at his sibling. "Do you think it's safe for us to leave?"

"I think the colonists can protect themselves until we return. For that matter, why can't you leave a few of your crew behind? You can get by without them."

The proposal had merit, Donovan realized. Almost all of *Liberator*'s systems were automated, and shipboard operations that once required three or four men to handle in conventional submarines were now performed by just one. Instead of a hundred and twenty men or more, only forty-five manned *Liberator*, forty-five of the best men in the Navy. Because so many of the ship's systems were computerized and roboticized, her crew was the best trained and best educated of any ever assembled. They were also older than the norm, and, until the war, better paid. While they were all specialists in their own right and their duties seldom overlapped, many had been taught the basics of other positions in the event of a manpower shortage. "You're on a roll, Pirate," he said.

"How so?"

"Two bright ideas in a row. Can your brain handle the strain?"

"You're just jealous because they weren't your ideas."

Chuckling, Donovan watched the point man cross a clearing. The simple fact they could engage in idle banter again made him happy. For a couple of months after the holocaust everyone had been understandably grim. Now that they'd found a new home and were rebuilding their lives, the crew and the colonists could laugh once again.

For another fifteen minutes the detail wound through the jungle in a generally westward direction. Birds were everywhere, as were insects of every size and description. Gorgeous butterflies seven inches across flitted from flower to flower. Beetles the size of a man's thumb crawled about on nearby limbs. Between the singing of the birds and the buzzing of the insects, a steady background chorus demonstrated the inherent vitality of the lush, primeval forest.

The point man unexpectedly halted and waited for them to catch up.

"What is it, Fitz?" Donovan inquired as they drew closer.

"I haven't seen a track since we left the spring. Do you want me to keep going in this direction?"

Donovan halted. "We might as well. It was too much to expect the things would leave a trail right to their den. They never have before."

"Yes, sir," Fitz said, and took off once more.

Charlie gazed up at the smoke pouring from the cone and made a clucking sound. "Do you ever worry about that sucker erupting?"

"Every day."

"Then why the hell did we settle down here?"

"Because Espiritu is ideal for our purposes. Not only is it one of the few uncontaminated islands we found, but there's also plenty of food and water," Donovan replied. "You know the reasons as well as I do." He began to trail after Fitz.

"I know. But the whole time we were getting everything organized, I kept hoping someone would come forward and point out we'd be wiser to select an island that won't blow its top in the next five, ten, or three hundred years."

"Why didn't you say something sooner?"

Pirate shrugged. "I didn't want to rock the boat, I guess. Everyone was so overjoyed at finally locating a place where we could live, I felt guilty about bringing it up."

"Well, let me put your mind to rest. In the first place, according to the records this volcano has been belching smoke for hundreds of years, since the arrival of the early Spanish explorers. In the second place, all the scientific studies conducted prior to the war indicated the molten core of the volcano is stable. The magma is about twenty miles below the surface, and the cone simply serves as a conduit to vent the built-up gases. As long as smoke keeps pouring out, we're safe."

Surprise prompted Charlie to do a double take. "I'm impressed. Since when did you become a volcano expert?"

"Since I started living with Alex. For your information, she was concerned about an eruption, too, and she spent days checking and rechecking all the data. Everything I just told you came straight from her mouth."

"Oh. Well, in that case I'll believe it."

"Thanks heaps."

The undergrowth became denser the farther the detail went. They were compelled to shoulder their way through thickets and fought a continual battle with hanging vines and exposed roots.

"I wish we'd brought along machetes," Charlie remarked.

Donovan nodded, wondering if the animals had deliberately taken a course over the most impassable terrain in order to discourage pursuit. The notion sparked a grin. He was probably attributing human qualities and levels of intelligence to beasts that operated on a purely instinctual level.

They drew slowly nearer to the imposing cone. Thankfully, the vegetation thinned considerably as they approached a low rise. Instead of heading over it, the point man bore to the right to go around.

The hunt provided a perfect opportunity for Donovan to reflect on what to do about the families in New York. After weighing the pros and cons, he reluctantly concluded he had no choice. *Liberator* must leave as soon as possible.

"You know," Charlie commented, "we should look at the bright side of all of this."

"What bright side?"

"All problems are relative, and a pack of man-eaters can't begin to compare with *Nemesis*."

The mention of *Liberator*'s enigmatic sister ship brought a torrent of bitter memories to Donovan's mind. First encountered in the North Pacific Ocean between Alaska and the Pacific Northwest, *Nemesis* had dogged *Liberator* for thousands of miles, playing a deadly game of cat and mouse. At first Donovan didn't know what to make of the mystery ship. It could run faster and dive deeper than *Liberator*, and whenever he tried to close in the phantom sub left him in its wake.

Only later did he learn a few pertinent facts. *Nemesis* turned out to be a German sub secretly constructed at a leased shipyard in Gdansk. The Greater Germany Defense Force, as the military forces of Germany became known after East and West Germany achieved total reunification, felt the need to flex its muscle on the world stage and did so by building a nuclear-powered submarine more sophisticated and more powerful than any previously known.

To add insult to the irony, the Germans obtained their keel and a partial hull from the United States after Congress in its infinite wisdom decided to deny the Pentagon the funds to complete construction of a second Omega-class sub. So, in effect, *Nemesis* became *Liberator*'s twin, her sister.

Nemesis also became the means used by the Fourth Reich to start World War Three. When the Russian hard-liners assumed power a series of minor confrontations between U.S. and Soviet units led to the call for a summit meeting of America's allies to work out strategies for dealing with the new Kremlin leadership. The defense ministers of the United States, Japan, the People's Republic of China, and even the newly reunited Germany met on a carrier in the Sea of Japan. *Nemesis* nuked the carrier.

Because neither the United States nor Russia knew *Nemesis* was the culprit, America blamed the Soviet Union and in no time at all tempers reached the boiling point. At long last the supreme insanity was unleashed on a breathless world. The Fourth Reich achieved its goal of provoking the war, then sat back to watch the superpowers slug it out.

Donovan discovered all this information much later. He had no idea whether the Fourth Reich survived the Armageddon it caused, but he doubted that the fanatics started the conflict without a contingency plan to ensure that the Reich emerged from the chaos in a position to become the dominant power on the globe. If it had survived, by now there should have been German broadcasts on the airwaves or reports of their activities elsewhere. Yet there hadn't been so much as a peep.

Except for *Nemesis*, of course. Donovan never did make contact with the German sub's crew. After a series of increasingly violent confrontations, *Liberator* finally succeeded in sinking her foe. Or so everyone believed. Donovan wanted to believe it, too, yet deep down a persistent doubt gnawed at him. After their final battle he'd wanted to search the vicinity for as long as it took to find concrete proof *Nemesis* was gone, but his crew took a vote and opted to return to Espiritu. He hoped—he prayed—they wouldn't regret their decision one day.

As for the rest of the world, there was little information to go on. Except for the shortwave transmissions from Pete and Sal, the United States was as silent as a tomb. So was the Soviet Union. A few scattered broadcasts had been received, one apparently from England, another from a Scandinavian country, and a third possibly from Turkey. The messages had been too short to pinpoint and disrupted by static. On top of that, the Scandinavian and Turkish transmissions were in languages none of the colonists spoke with any degree of fluency.

There *must* be more survivors out there, Donovan reflected. The nuclear blasts and the resultant firestorms had devastated the superpowers, and radiation insanity had claimed countless lives in other countries, but there still existed regions relatively untouched by the destructive forces unleashed when humankind presumed to play God with its own destiny. Espiritu was a case in point.

One of the reasons Donovan had worked so hard to establish a base of operations and start anew was his driving passion to make a difference, to salvage some semblance of civilization from the widespread ashes of the past. As far as he knew, no other American vessels survived. For that matter, *Liberator* enjoyed the distinction of being the premier military power on the planet. With such power came an awesome responsibility to use it wisely and compassionately. He intended to aid survivors wherever they might be found, and his men were all pledged to the same effort.

The more he thought about it, the more Donovan realized he'd made a mistake in not departing for New York City sooner. After all the speeches he gave about moral responsibility and duty, he'd failed to live up to his own words. Was it any wonder both Alex and Charlie expressed disappointment in his decision?

"A seashell for your thoughts, big brother?" Pirate remarked.

"The last of the big spenders," Donovan quipped.

"Seashells are more valuable than money right now," Charlie noted. "At least you can use them as ornaments or ashtrays."

"I was thinking about *Nemesis*," Donovan revealed.

"Again?"

"Can I help it if I think we made a mistake?"

"You're just paranoid, Tom. After so many years in the Navy you just naturally aren't comfortable unless there's an enemy to face."

Donovan glanced at his brother to see if Pirate was smiling, and was relieved to see him smirking broadly. "For a second there I thought you really meant that."

"Lighten up, Tom. Remember what Dad always said."

" 'A person is his own worst enemy,' " Donovan quoted.

"Exactly. I'm sure we'll come across enough threats out there without having to worry about those that are past history."

"I hope you're right about *Nemesis*," Donovan said, and dropped the subject.

They were almost to the rise. The point man was long since out of sight on the other side.

Charlie glanced over his shoulder, then leaned toward his brother and spoke softly. "What do you think of Betty Thompson?"

"Betty who?" Donovan responded with feigned disinterest.

"You know. The woman from San Francisco who lives with two kids on the north side of the village. She used to be a librarian before the war."

"Oh. You mean the widow whose husband was in the Marines?"

"That's her."

"The blonde who fills out a swimming suit better than anyone else on the island, excluding Alex?"

"Yeah. That's her, already. Have you spoken to her much?"

"A few times."

"So what do you think?"

"I think you could do worse."

"But she has children, Tom, and I don't know if I'm ready for responsibility like that."

"Did I miss something here? Have you proposed to her?"

Charlie blinked a few times. "No. Of course not. I hardly know her. I was just thinking of, you know, going to see her on a regular basis."

"So you haven't taken any moonlit strolls on the beach?"

"What kind of a question is that?"

Donovan opened his mouth to voice a witty rejoinder when from the far side of the rise came a shriek of terror.

Donovan immediately broke into a run, but he was already two strides behind his brother. He stayed on Charlie's heels as they rounded the rise on the right, listening to the shriek fade to a gurgling whine, the short hairs at the nape of his neck tingling. There was only one reason the point man would cry out like that, and he dreaded what they would find.

"Fitz!" Pirate bellowed. "Fitz! Answer me!"

There was no response.

In seconds they reached a point where they could see a tract of shoulder-high grasses and reeds, a strip of jungle beyond, and the volcano.

Fitz was nowhere in sight.

"Fitz!" Charlie yelled frantically.

Donovan saw the grasses thrashing violently thirty feet away, and nudged his brother. "There!" he cried, dashing toward the spot.

The thrashing abruptly ceased. Instead, the grasses and reeds bent and rustled in several directions at once as half a dozen or more of the mystery beasts fled.

"No!" Charlie yelled, and squeezed off a short burst, aiming at a line of shaking reeds off to the left. Whatever was in there simply kept going, vanishing into the trees before another burst could be fired.

With the rifle pressed to his shoulder Donovan barreled through the grasses and almost stumbled over the prone body in his path. He halted in midstride, taking in Fitz's torn pants and shirt and outflung arms in a glance, then scanned the field to ensure none of the things were nearby.

Charlie ran up, took one look, and closed his eyes. "Damn. Damn. Damn. I never should have let him get so far ahead."

The rest of the men pounded up.

"Go after the animals," Donovan ordered. "Don't get isolated."

Off ran the detail, their expressions reflecting their outrage at the attack.

Kneeling, Donovan gently turned the seaman over and scowled at the sight of Fitz's torn throat. Blood gushed from the rupture. As with Webber, whatever jumped Fitz had killed him before he could get off a shot. The Franchi lay inches from the crewman's right hand, one of the most lethal submachine guns ever made rendered totally worthless by the unseen creatures.

"He was a good man," Charlie said softly.

"And he's the last one those things are going to get," Donovan vowed. "We must devise a strategy for eliminating them permanently. When we get back I'm calling a meeting of all the colonists and I want you there."

"Did you happen to get a look at whatever did this?"

"No. You?"

"Just a glimpse of a hairy form, that was all."

Donovan closed Fitz's wide eyes and stood, thinking of how the colonists would take the news of the two deaths. This was the first major crisis they'd faced since arriving at their new home, and how they handled it would reliably gauge their ability to confront future difficulties.

"We have company," Charlie unexpectedly announced, gazing to the southeast.

Pivoting, Donovan recognized the approaching man by his bulk. No one else on Espiritu matched their resident hermit in sheer size. Six and a half feet tall, weighing close to two hundred and fifty pounds, all of it muscle, the newcomer would stand out on the most crowded street in any major city, provided any major cities still existed to stand out in.

"Morning, fellas. What's all the shooting about?" inquired the giant known as Baltimore Jack. A battered felt hat covered his sandy hair, a perfect match for his torn T-shirt and faded old khaki trousers cut off at the knees. He sported a bushy beard determined to take over his entire face and neck.

"Hello, Jack," Charlie greeted him.

Donovan simply nodded. He still didn't know quite what to make of the former wrestling star who had abandoned the ring to take up a simplistic life in the South Pacific. Alex and another crewman first discovered Jack hiding in the jungle, and the story the man told was incredible.

Baltimore Jack—or Randolph Scott Wayne, as his parents had christened him—was the World Wrestling Federation champ from 1997 through 2006. Rated as one of the ten most popular men in America by *People* magazine in 2005, his career hit the skids the next year when he fought the Russian champ in a televised bout broadcast around the globe.

Jack took on the Siberian Tiger at the Gorbachev Exposition Hall in Red Square, a match grandly billed as a historic stepping-stone in U.S.-Soviet relations. Hardliners in both countries loudly denounced the event as a farce but were unable to turn the tide of favorable public opinion. So, in front of five hundred million worldwide viewers, and on the Siberian Tiger's home turf, Jack employed a time-honored wrestling move known as the full-weight head slam halfway through the match and would have won then and there if not for a surprising development. He killed the Tiger.

An autopsy later revealed that the Siberian's neck snapped at impact, and the blame was placed on the unfortunate workers who erected the ring and stretched the mat too tight. The death caused an uproar in Russia, a national scandal of unprecedented proportions. (Some U.S. political analysts asserted that the disgraceful outcome of the bout directly led to the overthrow of the liberal Soviet president, but serious pundits scoffed at the idea.)

Baltimore Jack retired from the ring soon afterward. He took his millions and disappeared, and until he popped up on Espiritu most everyone had forgotten all about him.

Now the former wrestler halted and stared in shock at the dead sailor. "Good God. What happened?"

"We finally have some idea of what has been doing all the howling," Donovan said. "There's a pack of man-eaters running loose."

"Man-eating what?"

"That we don't know yet," Donovan said. "But I'd advise you to move into the village as soon as possible. I'll send two armed men to escort you if you want."

"And leave my house?" Jack responded in his deep voice. "No way, dude."

Donovan glanced at the volcano, but he couldn't see the Swiss-style A-frame chalet perched on the south slope from where he stood. He'd visited the house several times and admired the setup: a solar energy system backed up by a windmill provided ample power; a freshwater spring supplied mineral-rich water; and a genuine redwood deck afforded a sweeping vista of the island and the ocean. "I'm afraid I must insist."

Jack straightened. "Hey, this is *my* island."

"Don't start that again," Donovan said. The wrestler claimed to actually own Espiritu, claimed he purchased the island outright from the natives and relocated them on Tahiti, but he wasn't able to provide any supporting documentation.

"Why won't you believe me?"

"We've been all through this," Donovan told him. "And I'm not about to go into it again right now. Two men have been killed, and I'm not going to let anyone else die. Whether you like it or not, I'm in charge of operations here. So for your own safety I'm having you moved to the village."

"I won't go," Jack said stubbornly.

"Then I'll send ten men to drag you back."

"You would, wouldn't you?"

Donovan gestured at Fitz. "Damn it, use your head. Do you want to wind up like him?"

The wrestler stared intently at Donovan for a moment. "No, I guess I wouldn't," he stated, "but I'm an old hand at taking care of myself."

"Do you own any guns?"

"Of course not, man. Guns are for wimps."

"Do you own any weapons at all?"

"I've got a hunting knife and an axe."

"Not good enough," Donovan said, nodding at the body. "This man carried a submachine gun, and a fat lot of good it did him. I'm sorry, Jack. You must give me your word you'll temporarily move into the village."

"Temporarily, huh?"

"Until this problem has been eliminated."

Sighing, Baltimore Jack nodded. "All right. You've got my best interests at heart. I'll go along with you this time," he said, emphasizing the last two words.

"Thanks."

"How soon do you want me there?"

"Yesterday."

"On my way, then," Jack said. He gazed sadly at Fitz.

"Sorry about your man. I truly am." With that he turned and hastened off.

"Strange, strange man," Charlie commented.

"Every South Sea island must have at least one colorful character," Donovan mentioned absently while watching the giant depart. "It's traditional, I believe."

"Something about him bothers you, doesn't it?"

"Everything about him bothers me. He seems to think he's the lord and master of Espiritu and views the rest of us as trespassers. I can't help but think he'll give us a lot of trouble in the future."

"Cross that bridge when you come to it."

Donovan grinned. "Yeah. I guess you're right." He glanced toward the volcano and saw the remaining members of the detail returning on the double.

"Anything?" Pirate called out when they were still twenty yards away.

"No, sir," the sailor in the lead replied. "No sign of the things."

"Figures," Donovan muttered.

"We'll nail them. Don't worry."

Frowning, Donovan surveyed the jungle rimming the cone. How highly appropriate, he thought, that the jungles here were as unsafe as the rest of the world. In a certain sense, the war had transformed the entire planet into a toxic jungle where the only law was the survival of the fittest. Wildlife in the contaminated zones was universally hostile to all humans. Predators were more vicious than ever, and normally docile species were now savage. Even a lowly flock of gulls attacked *Liberator* at one point. Humankind wasn't safe anywhere. He'd foolishly believed the colonists were secure on Espiritu, but Nature had proven him wrong.

"Ready when you are."

Donovan turned to find the detail awaiting orders. He

pointed at two of the men. "I want the two of you to follow Baltimore Jack to his house. You're to make sure he packs and heads for the village within the hour. Is that understood?"

"Aye, Captain," acknowledged one of them.

"Off you go."

They jogged away.

Donovan knelt and looped an arm under Fitz's shoulders. "Give me a hand. We'll carry him back together."

"We can handle it," Charlie offered. "You don't need to bother."

His eyes narrowing, Donovan looked at his brother. "He was one of my men. I'll help."

In no time they lifted the hapless Fitz onto their shoulders and started tramping in the direction of the village. The going was exceedingly slow when they reached the denser tracks of jungle, and all of them were sweating profusely before they had covered five hundred yards. Periodically they stopped to rest, saying little, sobered by the reminder of their own fragile mortality. It took them three times as long to retrace their path than it had to chase the animals, and at long, weary last they shuffled from the vegetation and gazed in profound relief at the scores of huts spread out before them.

"We'll place the body in my hut for the time being," Donovan instructed them, starting forward.

Dozens of colonists were milling about, engaged in hushed conversations. They stared at the corpse in ill-concealed apprehension.

"The word must be spreading fast," Charlie remarked. "Almost half the village is there."

"And the rest will join them soon," Donovan predicted. "Which is just as well. It saves me the trouble of calling them all together for the announcement I'm going to make."

"About what?"

"I'd rather keep it as a surprise."

"You don't trust your own brother?" Charlie asked in mock horror. "What's this world coming to?"

Donovan spied several people conversing outside his hut. Alex was one. Beside her were Communications Officer Dave Jennings and Chief Engineer Smith. They saw the detail approaching and Alex hastened inside while the officers ran to meet him.

"Captain," Dave Jennings declared. "Who is it?"

"Seaman Fitz."

"Son of a bitch," Chief Smith said. "What happened, sir?"

"I'll fill everyone in shortly, Flazy," Donovan stated, using the nickname bestowed on the heavyset engineer by the crew.

Carl Smith, whose nickname stood for "fat and lazy," knew more about *Liberator*'s systems than any other man in the crew, with the possible exception of the ship's sterling helmsman, young Dave Hooper. Smith was a whiz when it came to nuclear propulsion systems, computers, and electronics in general. He'd even been consulted on crucial design decisions during *Liberator*'s construction. His expertise rated him the top engineering post on the top submarine in the entire U.S. fleet.

Communications Officer Jennings was extremely competent in his own right, although his main strength, in Donovan's estimation, was the unflappable emotional stability he projected on the bridge. No matter how severe the crisis, no matter how excited everyone else became, Jennings invariably maintained his cool. His calm, professional presence counted most when the chips were down.

Only one officer on *Liberator* could claim to be more self-possessed than Jennings, and that man was Donovan himself. He knew his mild temperament, as well as his proven adaptability and wide experience on submarines, had garnered him a post most sub commanders would have given their eyeteeth for. Donovan cut his own teeth on Los Angeles–class submarines, rising to the rank of captain and enjoying his first command in much less time than it took the average officer.

One of Donovan's men had advanced quickly through the ranks, too, though for entirely different reasons. That man was none other than his firebrand second-in-command, John Percy. Only thirty years old, Percy was brilliance personified where tactical operations were concerned. No one ever bested him at war games. His brilliance, however, was tempered by his impulsive, hotheaded nature. Percy would take risks other commanders shunned, and he was all too eager to wade into battle at the proverbial drop of a hat. When assigning Percy to Donovan, the brass had hoped Donovan's mild disposition would rub off on the younger man.

Now Donovan saw his executive officer hurrying toward him from the west. He twisted to look at the detail and announced, "Let's carry Fitz into my living room." They did so, gently depositing the body on the floor.

Alex came out of the bedroom with a green blanket in her hands. "We don't want the flies to get to him," she said, and covered the corpse.

Donovan straightened and massaged a kink in his lower back just as Percy entered. "Mr. Percy, I'm glad you're here."

"You are, sir?"

"Yes. I want you to take Mr. Jennings and Flazy on board *Liberator*."

"May I ask why, Captain?"

"Certainly," Donovan said, and realized he was the focus of attention for everyone in the room. "I want you to get *Liberator* ready to shove off. We're leaving for New York City in three hours."

God, she was beautiful.

Donovan stood on the topside bridge two stories above the foredeck and admired the contours of his ship, the most advanced nuclear submarine ever constructed by the United States, the ship once heralded as "the ultimate technological achievement" and "the pride of the U.S. Navy."

Liberator's teal-colored hull knifed through the blue-green waters of the South Pacific on a northeasterly bearing. Her titanium-composite hull was rated as the strongest ever built, able to withstand near misses from enemy torpedoes or cannons. Four hundred feet in length, she resembled nothing so much as a gigantic dolphin or porpoise. In fact, her advanced hydrodynamic design stemmed from decades of research into the aquatic capabilities of such cetaceans.

Even the bridge on which Donovan stood was completely hydrodynamic, with the same low, sloping profile as the ship. Teardrop shaped, with the broad end naturally facing the bow, the unique blister reduced resistance and afforded *Liberator* an extra five knots when running submerged. But it also had a drawback: spray from the bow in choppy water drenched anyone standing topside.

Today the Pacific Ocean was serene, and the occasional light spray that moistened Donovan's face felt refreshing instead of being a nuisance. He loved to head out to sea again after an extended stay ashore. The gentle motion of the sub under his feet, the salty breeze stirring his hair, and the prospect of new adventures waiting over the horizon always combined to give him an emotional kick like no other experience. He smirked at the thought. There *was* one other experience that always gave him an emotional jolt, but it was decidedly more sensual in nature and the two hardly deserved comparison.

Just standing there on top of such an amazing ship—the behemoth of submarines, as it were—was enough to imbue anyone with a sense of awesome responsibility, and Donovan never let himself forget he was in command of a vessel that qualified as the supreme military power on the planet.

Liberator's armaments were awesome. They included about three dozen Mark 70 long-range, laser-guided, acoustic-homing torpedoes, and two dozen or so Mark 97N nuclear missiles. Also incorporated into her defenses was the greatest advance in sub warfare, a laser able to disrupt electrical circuits on enemy craft at a range of 1,000 yards on the surface and 1,500 underwater. In addition, the laser could be employed as a probe to feed information into the ship's Cray-9 computer. Her more conventional weaponry consisted of five Walther PB AutoStrafe machine guns, any one of which could be fitted at a moment's notice to the special mount aft of the topside bridge.

Donovan glanced down at the hull, thinking of all the men below who were diligently going about their duties at spacious stations that would have made an old-time submariner drool with envy. Designed to be a home away from home, *Liberator* was almost luxurious in contrast to her predecessors. She was more like a seaborne colony. Her galley, sick bay, and library were huge. Every member of the crew had his own cabin, and the officers enjoyed the extra benefit of having their own heads and showers. Her compact computerized systems contributed greatly to the available extra space, as did one other factor.

Liberator's nuclear power plant took up much less space than earlier models. Just aft of amidships was her reactor room, where a Westinghouse NCS Superfluid Metal Coolant Reactor operated quietly and efficiently. According to Flazy, the reactor could run indefinitely on the fuel it had. And thanks to advances made over the primitive reactors built prior to the year 2000, it never came close to redlining.

Located aft of the reactor were *Liberator*'s three T7W General Dynamics steam turbines. Only two of them were on-line at any given time. The third was always maintained in reserve for emergencies or to replace an engine down for routine overhauls. Due to the efficiency of the heat-transfer mechanism on the nuclear-steam link, the reactor and turbines were able to propel the sub at a speed of sixty knots when operating at only two thirds of their peak rating.

Donovan affectionately patted the rail. If not for the fact that *Liberator* had been on a shakedown cruise under the North Pole when the war erupted, he wouldn't be alive to enjoy the sunshine and the thrill of sailing into the unknown.

A youthful voice intruded on his musing.

"Sir, a whale off the port bow."

Donovan glanced at the speaker. "A *whale*, Mr. Hooper?"

Helmsman Dave Hooper, the youngest member of the crew, nodded and lifted his left hand to point. "Yes, sir. Right there."

Amused but keeping a straight face, Donovan shifted his gaze to the indicated expanse of ocean and spied the animal approximately half a mile away. The distance was too great to permit identification, although he could tell the thing was enormous. Probably seeking others of its kind, he reasoned, and stabbed the bridge intercom button. "Mr. Jennings?"

"Yes, Captain?" the communications officer answered.

"Is the sonar operator asleep?"

Jennings never missed a beat. "Not to my knowledge, sir."

"Then perhaps you can explain to me why there's a whale the size of Moby Dick off the port bow and no one bothered to inform me sooner?"

"I'll check, Captain."

"You do that," Donovan said, and clicked off. He idly trained the binoculars on the whale, noting its broad back and a distinct dorsal hump, while waiting for Jennings to call back. He'd given strict orders that every contact, no matter how faint or questionable, was to be reported immediately, and he wouldn't tolerate a breach of discipline concerning such a crucial matter. What if the whale had been *Nemesis*?

The command structure enabled Donovan to delegate responsibilities efficiently. Communications, Jennings's department, oversaw Sensors (which included sonar, radar, the lasers and radio), Computers, and Research. Weapons Control, which was Executive Officer Percy's bailiwick, included the missile deck, the torpedo room, and the lasers when they were operating in the weapons mode. Reactor Control reported to the System Chief, Flazy. Overlapping areas were duly shared.

"We haven't seen many whales lately, Captain," Hooper commented.

"True," Donovan responded, watching a bushy spout spray from the animal's blowhole.

"All we ever see are sharks," Hooper went on in a conversational vein.

Shifting the binoculars a few degrees to the south, Donovan spied half a dozen large fins crisscrossing the surface, and he frowned. Hooper was right. Sharks,

sharks everywhere, constantly on the prowl. His brother had nearly been eaten by one during their last cruise.

The simple fact was that since the war the predators of the sea and land were more in evidence than ever before. In San Francisco the crew ran into wolves. In South America it had been jaguars. Wherever they went, they encountered new menaces.

Peter Fisher had a theory. He believed the animals were afflicted with the same radiation psychosis ravaging so many of the human survivors. The disease apparently stimulated the specific areas of the brain dealing with aggressive behavior, which explained why all predators were now more antagonistic and vicious and why even normally docile species were exhibiting uncharacteristic violence. The war had transformed the world into a jungle worse than the one on Espiritu.

A muted crackling came from the intercom speaker.

"Captain?"

"Yes, Mr. Jennings?"

"With apologies from the chief engineer, he was running a calibration check and took over the sonar station for a couple of minutes. He picked up the whale but didn't consider it important enough to bother you."

"Oh, he didn't, did he?"

"Yes, sir. Would you like me to relay a message to him?"

"Yes. Advise Flazy that he'd better not miss officer's call this evening or his ass will be grass."

"Roger, Captain."

Donovan straightened and heard a chuckle behind him. Discipline, it seemed, was going all to hell. With *Nemesis* hopefully disposed of, and with the Department of the Navy a historical footnote, the crew wasn't maintaining the same razor-edged performance it once had. What should he do about it? If he clamped down, they'd only become resentful. And he wouldn't blame them.

A new era had begun, an era in which armies and navies were nonexistent, in which the threat of global obliteration was gone, in which all the men wanted to do was get on with their lives as best they were able. It was enough that they'd voted to continue functioning as a Navy unit and to respect the old chain of command. If they had decided that enough was enough and opted to settle down permanently on Espiritu or somewhere else, there was nothing Donovan could have done to stop them. His authority now rested more on his personality and experience than his rank.

"What's this I hear about a whale?"

Donovan glanced down at the hatch and saw the love of his life climbing out. Smiling, he gave her a hand. "True enough. Off the port bow."

Alex moved to the rail and placed her right hand above her eyes to shield the sunlight. "Looks like a big one."

"Use these," Donovan suggested, removing the binoculars.

"What kind is it?" Alex wondered as she raised the glasses to her face.

"Beats me. I'm not a whale expert. You're our science officer. You tell me."

"Don't mind if I do," Alex said, and studied the huge animal for a while. "You know, I think it's a sperm whale."

"You mean like in *Moby Dick*?" Donovan responded in surprise.

Helmsman Hooper chuckled. "You must be psychic, Captain."

"Psychic?" Alex repeated without taking her eyes from the whale.

"We were just discussing the literary merits of Herman Melville," Donovan said with a straight face.

Hooper cackled.

"When will I learn?" Alex quipped.

Donovan leaned next to her and gazed out over the tranquil sea. At such lighthearted moments it was easy to forget the ravaged condition of the rest of the world, to almost pass the war off as a grisly figment of an overactive imagination. Almost, but not quite.

"Do you miss Charlie?" Alex casually inquired.

"Someone had to be in charge of the hunt for those maneaters. I'd rather it was him than one of the colonists."

"I noticed he didn't take the news you were leaving him behind very hard. Do you think Betty Thompson was the reason?"

Donovan stared at Alex, wondering if she was the one who was psychic. "You know about Pirate's interest in Thompson?"

"His interest, as you call it, is obvious. He's been ogling her for a couple of weeks now."

"Has anyone else noticed, you think?"

"Oh, just Betty and every other woman on the island."

"Just the women, huh?" Donovan said sarcastically.

Alex nodded, the binoculars bobbing in rhythm with her chin. "Women are more in tune to such things. They know when a man is planning to put the make on them, and they see when a guy is interested in another gal."

"Aren't you being just a bit chauvinistic?"

"Not in the least. Men are just more obvious when their hormones kick into overdrive."

Donovan glanced at Hooper, who snickered, then impulsively bent forward and gave Alex a peck on the cheek despite his personal pledge not to show affection in front of the crew. He didn't want to compromise her position as the only woman on board by emphasizing their romance.

"What was that for?" she inquired.

"General principles."

For all of ten seconds they sailed in silence.

"Wow!" Alex abruptly exclaimed.

"What is it?"

"I think the sperm whale is a seventy-footer."

"Is that big for this kind?"

"It's as big as sperm whales come and quite rare. Prior to the eighteen hundreds, before the whaling industry reached its zenith and whalers killed off untold thousands of right and sperm whales for their oil, specimens this size were common. But by 1900 there were few of the really giant ones left," Alex disclosed. "And even though America cut back on her whaling efforts, other countries took up the slack to the point where sperm whales were on the verge of extinction. It took an international effort by concerned marine biologists and environmentalists to save them."

"I had no idea your expertise extended to whales," Donovan commented good-naturedly.

"Remind me to show you my T-shirt sometime."

"T-shirt?"

"Yeah. My 'Save the Whales' T-shirt. I was born and raised in San Francisco, remember? When I was a kid my dad took me out time and again to see the whales. I can recall standing in the bow of a boat filled with gawking tourists and watching these great mammals swimming south on their annual migration to prime breeding waters. We would get so close I could almost reach out and touch them." Alex grinned. "Other girls went through a phase where they were in love with horses. I was in love with whales."

"This must be a real treat for you."

"It is." Alex lowered the binoculars and bestowed an affectionate smile on him.

Donovan returned her warm gaze, wishing they were alone, until the spell was broken by a polite cough from Helmsman Hooper.

"Excuse me, Captain."

"Yes?"

"It's the whale, sir."

Donovan looked at the young seaman. "What about it?"

"The thing has changed course, Captain."

A glance confirmed the observation. Not only had the giant creature altered its heading from practically due west, but it was now swimming powerfully and quickly directly toward *Liberator*.

Coincidence? Donovan wondered, and decided to find out. "Mr. Hooper, change our course to zero-nine-zero degrees."

"Aye, Captain. Zero-nine-zero it is."

Liberator responded superbly, smoothly cruising due east at a speed of only twenty knots, a gentle white spray foaming the bow.

Alex was watching the whale, the set of her jaw betraying her concern. "You're not thinking what I think you're thinking, are you?"

"Afraid so," Donovan said. "Let me have the binoculars."

She passed them over without comment.

Hoping he was mistaken, Donovan studied the leviathan. A quarter of a mile now separated the whale and the sub. He could see its great back clearly as it crested the surface, propelled by mighty up-and-down strokes of its enormous tail. "What's the top speed of a sperm whale?" he asked.

"About twenty-five knots, I believe. Maybe thirty for a whale that size."

"Then we can easily outrun it if need be," Donovan said. So far the creature had not changed course to compensate for *Liberator*'s new bearing. Maybe he was letting his imagination get the better of him.

As if deliberately wanting to prove him wrong, the whale angled to intercept the sub.

"Damn," Donovan said.

"Even the whales," Alex stated in disbelief.

The intercom suddenly sputtered to life.

"Captain?" Communications Officer Jennings said.

"Donovan here."

"Flazy asked me to relay an update."

"Is he done tinkering with the sonar equipment?"

"Oh, yes sir. The update concerns the whales."

Donovan stiffened. *"Whales?"*

"Yes, sir. Flazy reports two more whales over two thousand feet below *Liberator* and surfacing rapidly."

Donovan glanced at Alex, whose anxious expression told him she shared his apprehension, and barked a command into the microphone. "Sound Alert Stations, Mr. Jennings! Tell Mr. Percy to prepare to dive. Have Mr. Colgan handle the helm until Hooper is below."

"Yes, sir," Jennings dutifully responded.

Pivoting, Donovan indicated the hatch. "Down we go. You first, Mr. Hooper. Move it." He gazed at the sperm whale as the helmsman obeyed. "Do those things usually travel in packs?"

"Pods, not packs," Alex corrected him.

"How many can be in a pod?"

"The most sperm whales ever recorded in a single pod was several hundred."

"Hundred?" Donovan repeated, stunned, and gestured for her to hasten down the hatch. What if *Liberator* had stumbled into the middle of a pod? Outmaneuvering a lone whale was one thing; outmaneuvering dozens or hundreds was another. He scanned the horizon for more of the huge beasts and saw none, then followed Alex, closing the hatch behind them.

Alert Stations was blaring when Donovan strode across the bridge to his customary seat in a swivel chair located behind the helmsman's station.

Executive Officer Percy hastened over. "What is it, sir? Are we under attack?"

"I believe so," Donovan responded.

"A Russian ship again? Or *Nemesis* back from the grave?" Percy asked hopefully.

"Sperm whales."

Percy blinked a few times, then chuckled. "Very funny, sir. What is it *really*?"

"I'm serious, Mr. Percy," Donovan emphasized, and turned his chair to gaze at Jennings. "Put them on the screen."

"Aye, Captain."

"Whales?" Percy said softly, in the same manner as he might say the word *Martians*.

Donovan faced forward again, his right elbow resting on the chair arm, studying the holographic wonder that served as the tactical eyes and ears of *Liberator*.

The screen, or Cyclops, as it was commonly designated, contained the most advanced technology on the ship. The system took all information supplied by Sensors, including sonar, radar, and UHF, and created an amazingly realistic three-dimensional image of the sub and the surrounding environment. Derived from the title Cycle Optics, Cyclops visually depicted the condition of the sea, the subsea terrain, and anything on the surface in shimmering blue and green light that seemed to hover in the air in front and partly on both sides of the captain's post.

Now, as Donovan watched, three icons materialized, one for each whale, accurately presented in relation to their distance from *Liberator* and their current speed. The pair approaching from below were smaller than the giant on the surface, but there was no doubt all three were converging on the same point. "Take her down, Mr. Percy."

The executive officer had recovered from his initial incredulity. "Aye, Captain," he said, and hurried to his own station. "Dive! Dive!"

Donovan suppressed a grin at Percy's enthusiasm. He glanced to his right at Alex, who was standing quietly regarding Cyclops, a forlorn aspect to her countenance. "What's wrong?"

"This hits home hard, Tom. I mean, wolves, sharks, and jaguars I can understand. Even the attack by those gulls makes perverted sense since Alfred Hitchcock gave them the idea."

"But?" Donovan prompted, unable to suppress a second grin.

"But whales never go out of their way to attack humans unless they're being attacked themselves. If the radiation insanity affects them, then there isn't a single species we can trust. Dogs. Cats. Cockroaches. Cows. You name it, they might try to kill us."

Donovan tried to envision a herd of rampaging cows and couldn't. "There's hope for the world. Your brother is working on an antidote for the radiation insanity."

"He's trying, but Pete doesn't even know what *causes* the disease. I'd say a cure is a long ways off."

Donovan had to postpone contemplating that distressing thought because of an announcement by Percy.

"Flooding the main ballast tanks, Captain. Fifteen degrees down angle on the diving planes."

Nodding, Donovan glanced at his helmsman's back. "Mr. Hooper, level off at two hundred feet."

"Will do, sir."

The three whales were still rapidly angling toward *Liberator*. Those below the ship were moving faster, perhaps due to the added momentum their natural buoyancy gave them, but the huge one sighted first was nearer, slightly over nine hundred feet away.

"We won't need to torpedo them, will we?" Alex asked.

"Not if it can be helped," Donovan said. "I'd rather not waste one on a rabid whale."

"Not funny, lover."

"Wasn't trying to be," Donovan said, performing calculations in his head. *Liberator* would level off in ten seconds, allowing more than enough time for the sub to achieve full speed before the whales could reach her.

"Captain," Jennings declared. "Sonar reports more whales."

"Range and number?"

"Four whales, sir, heading toward us at twenty knots. They're directly astern at a range of three thousand feet."

"Advise Sonar I want to be informed the second they pick up more whales."

"Yes, sir."

"Leveling off at two hundred feet," Hooper stated.

"All ahead full."

"All ahead full it is, Captain."

Leaning forward, Donovan watched the whales fall farther and farther behind as *Liberator* went faster and faster.

"Sixty knots, sir," Hooper disclosed half a minute later.

"They'll never catch us now," Donovan said, beginning to relax. He looked at Alex. "Your whales are safe and sound for the time being."

"Do I detect a note of reservation in your tone?"

"A little," Donovan admitted. "Those creatures are a threat to every boat in the South Pacific. If I had a way to do it without using torpedoes, I would have sent them to the bottom."

"You're more bloodthirsty than I thought. Except for ours, there aren't any boats left in the South Pacific. None that we know of, anyway. And the odds of other survivors bumping into the pod are remote. This is a big ocean."

"I hope you're right."

"Besides, if these whales have the radiation sickness, then other whales probably do. We certainly can't wipe out every last one."

"Captain, all of the whales except the biggest one have broken off the chase," Jennings said.

"Persistent devil," Donovan remarked, staring at the diminishing icons on the screen, and thought of a question to ask. "Alex, refresh my memory. How do whales locate other whales and prey?"

"Through their sense of hearing. Their vision isn't very keen and their sense of smell not much better. But their hearing is exceptional. They can hear a ship's engines from a mile away. Some whales make squeaking noises and other sounds, then listen to the echoes to determine distances."

"So those sperm whales must have homed in on *Liberator*'s cavitation sounds," Donovan speculated, referring to the noise produced by a propeller churning water at high speed.

"That would be my guess. Why?"

"Just curious."

"Captain, more whales," Communications Officer Jennings interrupted them.

"Not again," Donovan muttered, gazing at Cyclops. He saw them at the same moment Jennings elaborated.

"Seven whales off the starboard bow at a range of four thousand yards. They're on a bearing of two-nine-zero degrees."

"Heading toward us," Donovan concluded. "Okay. Two can play at this game. Mr. Hooper, bring us to a heading of one-eight-zero degrees. We'll swing around our aquatic cousins."

"Aye, Captain. One-eight-zero degrees."

Donovan turned to the love of his life again. "Tell me. How far apart can the members of a pod be spread?"

She shrugged. "Oh, over a couple of miles."

"Terrific."

Percy came over to stand by the swivel chair. "I can't believe we're running from a bunch of dumb animals, sir," he remarked.

Donovan flinched and pretended he hadn't heard, knowing how his feistier half would react.

"True whales may not be as intelligent as dolphins, Mr. Percy," Alex said stiffly, "but they're far from being simply dumb animals." She emphasized those last two words distastefully. "They're loving, devoted parents, and very sociable creatures. They demonstrated the resourcefulness to adapt superbly to a life in the sea and flourished for millions of years before humankind decided to exterminate them for oil, meat, and ambergris—"

"Amber what?" Percy interrupted, and received a scathing look that implied he might well be the world's only living Neanderthal.

"Ambergris, the best known substance for making perfumes retain their scent. Sperm whales, you see, eat giant squids. Giant squids have beaks," Alex explained as if instructing a first grader in elementary biology. "The whales can't digest these beaks, which collect in their digestive tract and become a sticky, dark, foul-smelling gook called ambergris. When the whales are cut open, the ambergris is removed and used to make perfume. Sometimes the whales just spit gobs of it out, sort of like a cat spitting out a hair ball, and it's gathered up."

Percy appeared shocked. "Let me get this straight. Before the war, women went around wearing whale puke on their faces?"

"That's a crude way of putting it," Alex said. "Essentially, though, you're correct."

The executive officer shook his head in amazement.

"And I've always *liked* perfume."

Alex stared at the screen. "Our species always was notorious for killing anything and everything if there was a profit to be made along the line."

"Look, Alex," Percy said, "I'm sorry if I've offended you. I made a stupid comment and I apologize. Are we still friends?"

"Of course. I never let masculine stupidity faze me."

Percy leaned down and whispered in Donovan's ear, "She must keep you on your toes, sir." Then he straightened, smiled at Alex, and walked off.

"What did he say?" she asked.

"He said I'm a lucky man," Donovan fibbed to preserve crew relations.

"He did?" Alex said, grinning. "Maybe there's hope for him, after all."

Donovan noticed that the last group of whales was much farther away and glanced at Jennings. "Distance to those seven whales?"

"Close to five thousand yards, Captain."

"This is like driving a sports car at a bumper car concession," Donovan joked. "They'll never get close enough to touch us."

"More whales," Jennings announced crisply. "Lots of them, sir. Six are surfacing from below, heading straight for us. There are four to starboard and three portside." He paused. "Now Sonar reports five more closing from behind."

"What the hell," Donovan said, coming out of his chair. There were whales all over the screen, dozens of them, with more icons popping up every second, and each and every one was heading toward the sub.

"Good God," Alex breathed. "We must be in the very middle of the pod!"

Charlie listened to the pounding of hammers and the rasping of saws on wood and surveyed the bustle of activity taking place on the south side of the village. Practically every colonist was on hand, with the majority busily engaged in erecting a crude but serviceable fence that would completely enclose the village by nightfall. A sense of urgency animated many of the faces while frank anxiety etched worry lines on others.

"It's going well, sir."

The comment drew Charlie's attention over his right shoulder to the four crewmen standing a few feet away. Seamen Wayne, Richards, Kent and Parker were wearing their uniforms and carrying Franchis slung over their shoulders. In addition, all four had .45-caliber pistols strapped around their waists and survival knives on their opposite hips. Clipped to their belts near the small of their backs were transceivers. "Yeah, it is, Mike," he answered Seaman Richards. "We'll have the fence done in time, no problem."

"You mean *they'll* have the fence done in time," Seaman Richards corrected him. A lean, muscular man who sported a neatly clipped beard and mustache, Richards was the best shot on *Liberator* next to Charlie. "All we're doing is standing around and watching. I feel sort of useless."

"So do I, sir," Seaman Wayne chimed in. The youngest of the four men comprising the gunnery detail, his curly black hair spilled out from under his white cap.

"We can't very well guard the colonists and chop down trees at the same time, now can we?" Charlie responded.

None of the men bothered to give so obvious an answer.

"Believe me, you won't feel useless by tonight," Charlie promised. "Not if those things come back."

"Do you think they will, sir?" asked Seaman Parker, a mousy crewman who wore glasses.

Charlie faced front. "I don't know. And cut out with the 'sir' stuff until my brother gets back. I'm not a stickler for discipline like Tom."

"But you *are* the Chief Gunnery Officer, sir," Kent mentioned. The biggest of the quartet, he pumped weights daily. "The captain ordered us to treat you accordingly, so like it or not, sir, you're stuck with the rank."

"Lucky me," Charlie quipped.

"I wonder where the ship is by now?" Wayne commented.

"About two hundred miles from Espiritu," Charlie guessed. "My brother is probably standing on the topside bridge with the wind in his hair and Alex by his side." He paused, then said seriously, "Lucky him."

"Sir?" Seaman Richards said.

"Yeah?"

"King Kong to port."

Pivoting, Charlie saw their moody hermit approaching. "Baltimore Jack," he greeted him cordially.

"I came to say good-bye," the former wrestler stated firmly.

Charlie folded his arms across his chest, thinking what he wouldn't give for a body like that. Betty Thompson would be putty in his hands. "Going somewhere?"

"Back to my house."

"Oh?"

"Yep. Now that your bro has taken off, I'm not about to stay here. I like my privacy."

"Tom gave specific directions for you to stay in the village until the animals are taken care of."

Baltimore Jack frowned and gazed off at the distant blue sea, his bronzed physique resembling a statue. "Between you and me, Charlie, your bro tends to get carried away with himself. I'm not in the military, and I resent having to take orders."

"That's too bad," Charlie said sweetly.

Jack looked at him. "Why?"

"Because the only way you're going back to your house is over my dead body."

A hint of menace touched Jack's eyes. "Are you threatening me?"

"Not at all. I wouldn't want to commit suicide," Charlie said, grinning. "But Tom left me in charge. All the colonists agreed to the arrangement—"

"I didn't," Jack interrupted.

"Really? I don't recall you speaking up when Tom called for objections to the idea."

Jack shrugged. "I didn't want to rock the boat."

"More likely you didn't want to draw attention to yourself because you planned all along to head for your house as soon as my brother left."

The corners of Baltimore Jack's lips curled upward. "Maybe I did, maybe I didn't. But I am going home whether you like it or not."

"I've known stubborn guys in my time, but you take the cake," Charlie said. He motioned at the four crewmen. "If you try leaving, the five of us will have to stop you."

"Are you kidding? I've been in ten-man tag team bouts. I can take you guys with one hand tied behind my back."

To Charlie's surprise, Seaman Richards stepped forward.

"No you can't," the bearded crewman said.

"And why not?" Jack responded arrogantly.

Richards grinned and patted the hilt of his survival knife. "Because I fight dirty."

For a few moments no one spoke. Baltimore Jack digested the revelation in somber silence. Finally he expelled a breath and nodded at Richards.

"You would, wouldn't you?"

"Without any hesitation whatsoever."

The wrestler glanced at Charlie. "Apparently I'm staying in the village longer than I'd anticipated. But I protest my treatment in the strongest terms. When your brother gets back, we're all going to sit down and have a long heart-to-heart about freedom and military dictatorships." So saying, he wheeled and walked off.

Seaman Richards waited until Jack was out of hearing before making a comment. "That guy is a few bricks shy of a load, if you get my drift."

"I wouldn't say so to his face if I were you," Wayne said.

"Forget about him for the time being," Charlie told them. He was about to say they had more important matters to discuss when he spied Betty Thompson and her two children walking past a hut thirty yards away, heading from south to north. "Wait here for me," he declared impetuously, and hastened to intercept them.

The former librarian wore jeans and a faded red blouse. Holding her left hand was her eight-year-old daughter, Melanie, and tugging on her right was her six-year-old son, Stevie. Both the kids wore shorts and shirts.

Charlie came up on them from the rear and heard the boy pleading with his mother.

" . . . for a little while. Please, Mom. Timmy says he can go. Please. Can I, huh?"

"No," Betty replied.

"Why not?" Stevie asked petulantly. "Timmy and I will only stay an hour."

"You're not going to play on the beach and that's final. I doubt very much whether Timmy's mother gave permission for him to go, and even if she did, you're not. Everyone is supposed to stay in the village until further notice."

"But nothing will eat us. It's the daytime."

"We have no idea what's out there. You're staying put, young man, until Charlie says it's safe to do otherwise."

"Ahhhh, he's no fun," Stevie groused.

"Charlie is very nice. He's just doing his job. You can't blame him."

Deciding to speak up before Betty realized he was there and suspected him of spying, Charlie cleared his throat and took advantage of the cue. "I wish everyone was as understanding as you are."

Betty halted and looked at him in surprise. Melanie displayed casual disinterest. Stevie's eyes fired nuclear missiles.

"Charlie. I didn't hear you come up."

"Sorry. Didn't mean to startle you."

Stevie jabbed a finger at Charlie's chest. "When can Timmy and me go to the beach?"

"Not until it's safe."

"When will that be?"

Charlie bestowed his most kindly expression on the boy. "Not until we catch whatever is out there."

"Why haven't you caught it yet?"

"We're trying," Charlie assured him, thinking it was too bad the world had been blown all to hell because the boy would make an excellent prosecution attorney some day.

"Catch it soon. Mom says I can't go to the beach until you do."

"I'll do my best."

Betty gave her son's arm a shake. "That's enough, Stevie. I don't want you pestering him."

"I don't mind," Charlie said.

"I'm heading home to make some sandwiches for the crew working on the fence. Care to tag along?" Betty asked.

"Don't mind if I do."

Stevie had something to say about that. "You should go catch the monster so I can go to the beach."

"It's not a monster," Charlie said pleasantly as they strolled toward the Thompson hut.

"How do you know?"

"Our problem is a pack of wild animals, nothing more."

"Then you should catch them quick."

"We will."

"When?"

Betty laughed self-consciously. "Stevie, I told you not to bother Charlie. If anyone can catch those things, he can. Why, I bet you didn't know he's an expert shot."

Stevie gave Charlie a glance that implied the boy doubted whether his mom's friend could nail the broad side of a barn with a bazooka at point-blank range. "Oh, yeah?"

"He won the U.S. Navy's pistol championship two years running," Betty elaborated.

The boy's interest perked up. He studied Charlie for a moment, then said, "You don't look like you know much about guns."

"Stevie!" Betty said. "That's not nice."

"How would you like a demonstration?" Charlie asked.

Stevie pointed at the Franchi slung over the younger Donovan's left shoulder. "With that?"

"No," Charlie said, tapping the Colt on his right hip. "With this."

"When?" Stevie inquired eagerly.

Glancing around, Charlie discovered there were few colonists in their immediate vicinity. He spotted a convenient coconut palm twenty yards to the northeast and halted. "How about right now?"

Betty and the children stopped. "Here?" she said skeptically.

"Why not?" Charlie responded. Here was a perfect opportunity to make a favorable impression on the boy, and he didn't want to let it pass. "I won't hit any innocent bystanders. I promise."

Grinning, Betty looked to the right and left. "What will you shoot?"

"Coconuts," Charlie said, pointing at the tree he'd selected. He glanced at Stevie. "How about if I knock a couple of coconuts off? Would that convince you I'm a good shot?"

Stevie squinted at the tree in question. "You sure you can hit them from here?"

"Watch me." Charlie drew the pistol.

"What kind of gun is that?" the boy asked.

"A Colt Stainless Steel Government Model forty-five. I like it because all the critical parts and major components are forged stainless steel, which is how it got its name, making the gun very rugged. It also has high-profile combat sights, which are a must in a tight situation."

"Is that a revolver?"

"No, it's an automatic pistol."

"What's the difference?"

"A revolver has a cylinder, a pistol doesn't. You cock it by pulling back on the slide, like so," Charlie explained, and did so to illustrate the procedure.

"Wow. You do know a lot about guns," Stevie said, duly impressed. "My dad knew a lot about guns, too."

"I'll bet he did."

"He was a Marine, you know."

Charlie, without gazing at the boy's mother, intuitively felt her eyes studying him. "I know."

"He could beat up anybody."

"Marines are tough," Charlie said.

"Have you ever beat anybody up?"

"Once or twice. But I don't make it a habit to go around punching people."

"Why not? You're a soldier."

"And soldiers are in the business of saving lives. A good soldier only fights when he's attacked. I'll bet your dad never hurt anyone unless they were trying to hurt him or someone he cared for."

"He kicked our dog once when it chewed up his combat boots."

Charlie chuckled and looked at Betty, pleased to note a hint of affection in her eyes. Their tender moment was abruptly punctuated by a yawn from the daughter.

"How long are we going to stand here?" Melanie asked in sincere boredom.

"Not long," Charlie said, and adopted a two-handed grip on the Colt, his legs spread in the traditional shooter's stance. He sighted carefully on a coconut, taking extra time, keenly wanting to impress the boy. Deep down, he also wanted to impress Betty Thompson with his prowess. He might not be a rough-and-ready leatherneck, but he was a military man and undoubtedly possessed some of the same martial traits she had so admired in her husband. Not that he thought he could replace the man in her heart. He only wanted her to care for him in his own right.

"What's the holdup?" Stevie asked.

Charlie stroked the trigger twice, the big .45 booming and bucking, and the coconut jumped like an airborne jackrabbit until gravity took over. Pleased at his performance, he straightened.

"Awesome," Stevie declared. "You're a great shooter, Mr. Donovan."

"Call me Charlie, please."

"Do it again."

Betty shook her head. "That's enough for now. We have sandwiches to make, remember?"

"Ahhh, gee, Mom."

"Your mom is right," Charlie said. "I'll take you out some day and we'll target practice together."

Stevie beamed excitedly. "You mean it?"

"Yep. If it's okay with your mother."

The boy hugged his mom's leg. "Can I? Can I go shooting with Charlie?"

"I suppose it would be all right."

Charlie detected hesitancy in her voice. "Is something wrong?"

"No. Not at all." Betty's expression became sheepish. "It's just that I've never been very fond of guns."

"But you married a Marine," Charlie said, stunned by the revelation.

"I married Lou because he was tender at heart, a man who could be as hard as nails on the job and yet totally loving toward me. He knew how I felt about guns and always kept his under lock and key."

Charlie quickly holstered the Colt, wishing he could find a hole and crawl into it. Of all the lamebrained, idiotic stunts he'd ever pulled, showing off for her qualified as the dumbest.

"Nothing personal," Betty added.

"Hey, look," Melanie stated, pointing to the southwest.

Turning, Charlie saw his gunnery detail jogging toward him. He assumed they'd heard the shots and come to investigate. "It was only me," he announced when they were close enough.

"You, sir?" Seaman Richards responded as the quartet slowed and stopped.

"The shooting," Charlie said lamely.

73

"That's not why we're here."
"Then why?"
"It's Baltimore Jack. We just saw him going into the jungle."

This can't be happening! Donovan thought furiously as close to four dozen whales materialized on the Cyclops display, the icons spread out in all directions from *Liberator*. The majority were already within two thousand yards of the ship, but they should have been detected much, much sooner. The ship's state-of-the-art sonar could easily pick up targets ten miles out. So why the hell were the whales popping up out of nowhere, so to speak, at such dangerous ranges? "Mr. Jennings, contact Flazy. Tell him we have a sonar malfunction and it must be fixed immediately."

"Yes, sir."

"Mr. Hooper, let's get out of here before those whales hem us in," Donovan said, studying the screen to determine the fastest route out of the pod. There were so many whales now, and the distances between them so slight, that evading the beasts would be difficult.

Another icon suddenly blinked on, representing a large sperm whale less than five hundred yards below the ship. The creature was reducing the range rapidly.

"Left full rudder," Donovan barked. "Ahead flank."

"Aye, Captain," Hooper replied.

Liberator maneuvered flawlessly, executing the hard turn and swiftly leaving the whale behind. Others appeared directly ahead.

"Slow to one half."

"One half it is."

Donovan saw three whales on his port quarter and

compensated. "Right twenty degrees rudder." It gave him a creepy feeling to be surrounded by deranged giants of the deep intent on destroying his ship. He calmed his nerves and applied logic to their dilemma. What possible harm could whales do to the most advanced nuclear sub ever constructed? "Sperm whales have teeth, right?" he asked Alex.

"Yep. They're the only big whales that do. Huge teeth, eight inches long, all in the lower jaw."

"Just the lower?"

"Yes. The teeth fit into holes in the upper jaw. Sperm whales need them to kill their favorite food, giant squid."

"*Liberator* is a damn sight harder than a lousy squid."

"Oh. I see what you're getting at. No, I doubt the whales will try to bite the sub. They'll probably try to ram us."

"Flesh and bone against a titanium-composite hull. How much damage could they do?"

"Hard to say. But many a sperm whale has turned on the catcher boats pursuing it and used its huge forehead as a battering ram. Sometimes they've even gone after the whaling ship. That's how Moby Dick sank the *Pequod*."

"The what?"

"Ahab's ship."

"A wooden vessel," Donovan commented. His main concern was whether an onrushing sperm whale could generate enough force upon impact to cause a crack in the ship's watertight integrity. Any breach of the hull, no matter how slight, would cripple *Liberator*. Lacking repair facilities, she would never be able to dive again, and if the crack was below her normal waterline, she might not even be able to stay afloat.

Intently studying the holographic images, Donovan spied a gap in the ring of monstrous mammals. "Mr. Hooper, do you see that opening to the northeast?"

"Yes, sir."

"Go for it. Put the pedal to the metal."

Hooper promptly steered the ship on a course of zero-four-five degrees.

"Look!" Alex exclaimed.

Donovan saw them, too. A pair of whales, one on the right and one on the left, on an intercept heading. If *Liberator* reached the gap before the whales cut her off, she'd be free and clear. The pair were only doing twenty knots, but they were closer to the opening. It would be nip and tuck. "Sound off on the two nearest whales, Mr. Jennings."

"The one to starboard is ninety-five yards away, the one on the port side only fifty."

"In ten-yard increments, if you please."

"Eighty-five and forty, Captain."

Everyone on the bridge realized the magnitude of the risk they were taking, and all eyes were glued to the screen in breathless anticipation.

"Seventy-five and thirty."

Donovan focused on the portside behemoth, his fingers digging into the arms of his chair. The icons were so close they were almost touching. In another second *Liberator* attained the gap, and suddenly the entire ship shuddered ever so slightly. He felt his chair tremble and recalled a similar experience, an earthquake measuring 4.1 on the Richter scale that struck when he was in Los Angeles five years before the war.

"We've been hit," Jennings announced.

"Damage report," Donovan ordered.

In moments *Liberator* was past the whales and heading for clear water.

"Mr. Hooper, maintain flank speed until I say otherwise. We're not slowing until there isn't a single whale on the screen."

"Yes, sir."

"Captain," Jennings stated, "we have no reports of any damage. The computer indicates the impact point as just aft of the missile deck."

"Nowhere near the rudder," Donovan said in relief. As he watched the screen, the holographic display shifted, blurred, then clarified with startling intensity. Suddenly all the whales were properly depicted to the rear of the ship, a few still in vain pursuit, some as far away as seven miles. "What was that?"

"Flazy must have fixed the sonar equipment," Alex speculated.

A couple of minutes later her supposition was verified when the chief engineer sheepishly approached the captain's station, a wan grin plastered on his fleshy features.

"This had better be good," Donovan said.

"It was a simple mistake, Captain," Flazy stated. "Could have happened to anyone."

"You're the last one I'd expect to make excuses for shabby performance. What the hell happened?"

"Well, you remember the calibration check I ran a short while ago?"

"I don't have amnesia."

"Yeah. Obviously not," Flazy said, glancing self-consciously at Alex. "I ran the check because the sonar operator reported a few fuzzy returns, but I didn't find anything wrong."

"Then what happened? Why didn't we pick up the rest of the pod when we should have?"

The chief engineer tightly clasped his hands together. "For a proper calibration test every piece of equipment must be set in the calibration mode. The BAT-9, the CS-14, the R-19, the whole works."

"Tell me something I don't know," Donovan said curtly. The BAT-9 was the ship's multifunctional sonar system, including the active and passive operations. Both relied on an enormous dome located in the bow, a transducer twenty-four feet in diameter. The CS-14 was a separate computer system from the sub's Cray-9. Its sole purpose was to amplify and analyze underwater noises. The R-19 was the key component in the passive system. Donovan possessed a basic working knowledge of each.

Flazy flinched as if from a physical blow. He took a deep breath and declared, "When the calibration test was over, someone forgot to turn the power control dial to the maximum setting."

"Someone?"

"I thought Seaman Hanning would adjust the dial when I was done, and he assumed I did."

"Thought? Assumed?" Donovan repeated, harshly accenting each word.

"It won't happen again, Captain," Flazy said quickly.

"You can bet on that," Donovan stated. Standing, he brushed past the flustered engineer and stepped to the communications station. "Mr. Jennings, I want to address everyone on board."

"Aye, Captain." Jennings flicked the necessary toggle switches to pipe the message to every speaker on the ship. "Ready when you are," he said, and handed over a microphone.

"This is the captain speaking," Donovan began. "Effective immediately, all hands will make an extra effort to adhere to proper procedure in the performance of their duties. It has come to my attention that many of us have become somewhat lax in recent weeks. This won't be tolerated.

"I know the war is over. I know many of you believe *Nemesis* has been destroyed. And I know our laid-back life-style on Espiritu is hardly conducive to maintaining a military frame of mind. But we can't afford to let down our guard for an instant. There are still plenty of dangers lurking out there, and if we're not extremely careful we might never see our island retreat again. We'll go by the book at all times. Now let's knuckle down and get to New York in one piece."

Jennings wore an inscrutable expression when he took the mike back.

"Any comments?" Donovan asked.

"I suppose this means the men can't work on their suntans topside during duty hours?" Jennings responded with a straight face.

Grinning, Donovan started to turn. "You missed your calling, Dave. You should have been a stand-up comic."

"Then I wouldn't have survived World War Three."

Alex eyed Donovan critically as he took his seat, but she refrained from speaking.

"I'm sorry, Captain," Flazy said. "I guess I'm as guilty as the next man of not staying as sharp as I should. In all the years I've been an engineer, I've never made a boneheaded mistake like that before."

"You're forgiven. Just make sure it doesn't happen again."

"It won't." Flazy nodded at Alex, pivoted, and walked off, his gaze averted from the crewmen he passed.

Resting his right elbow on the chair arm, Donovan placed his chin in his hand and waited for the inevitable reproof. He noticed with satisfaction the pod was much farther astern.

At last Alex voiced her opinion. "You were a little hard on him, weren't you?"

"No. His negligence could have cost us dearly."

"Could have, but didn't."

Donovan looked at her. "It doesn't make a difference that we came through unscathed. We should never have let ourselves be caught in such a situation in the first place. Had our sonar been functioning properly, we'd have detected the whales much sooner and taken appropriate evasive action. Flazy knows he did wrong."

"Then why did you have to rub his nose in it?"

"It's my job."

Alex nodded once and made a sniffing noise. "The military mentality."

"You seem to be forgetting a few things. First, this is a military vessel. Second, the crew members are all career military men."

"Were, you mean. The U.S. Navy no longer exists."

"Doesn't matter. As far as we're concerned, we *are* the Navy. Our own Navy. Or the Espiritu Royal Navy, if you want. But any way you look at it, the simple fact remains we are a military organization. Without discipline and adherence to proper procedure, our performance goes all to hell. We can't mesh effectively as a unit unless we correctly do our duties individually. Every man must do his job, and do it well," Donovan said, and went on quickly when she opened her mouth to interrupt. "You're upset because I got on Flazy's case. Yet as it was, I went easy on him. In the old days there were sub commanders who would have put him on report and punished him for his oversight."

Alex finally got in a word. "Too bad flogging isn't allowed," she said dryly.

"Don't you see how unfair you're being? You know as well as I do the magnitude of the problem we're facing in trying to rebuild the world from scratch. We've already had to contend with a Russian sub, *Nemesis*, a Panamanian dictator, pirates, and other menaces. If I'd let the men slack off, let their skills atrophy, let them violate procedure with impunity, do you really think we'd still be here today?"

"Probably not."

"Then I rest my case."

A few awkward moments of silence followed.

"I didn't mean to blame you personally," Alex said. "I thought you were going overboard, but now I understand the reason. Maybe I was just taking out my resentment on the military in general because it was the military-industrial complexes of the superpowers that destroyed our world."

"Blame the politicians. They were the ones who controlled the war machines."

"Yes, but the generals gave the final orders and the troops in the trenches pressed the buttons that launched the missiles."

"They were soldiers following orders."

"Which brings us back to the military mentality. I could never have pressed a button knowing I was unleashing a destructive force capable of leveling a city and killing millions of innocent people," Alex said, then blinked when she saw his lips compress and realized she'd inadvertently hurt his feelings. Twice since the war Donovan had fired nuclear missiles at inhabited sites, once at the white-shirt stronghold in San Francisco and once at a pirate base in the South Pacific. He'd done so only as a last resort and to save countless lives, but the deeds weighed heavily on his soul.

"Sometimes we must do things we don't like to do," Donovan said softly. "I know that's not much of an excuse, and it doesn't justify the destruction of civilization. Those soldiers who let the missiles fly were doing their duty. Any personal feelings they had were suppressed. The essence of the military mentality, as you call it, is obedience to higher authority. They simply had a job to do and they did it."

"I understand," Alex said, choosing her words carefully, "but I think blind obedience to any authority is a dangerous practice. Isn't that how dictatorships get started?"

"Yes," Donovan conceded. "That's why, under ideal conditions, the military is always accountable to wise politicians who have the best interests of their people at heart."

Alex seemed to gaze into the distance. "Idealism died with the planet."

"What about us? What about our plans for forging a new society? Don't we count?"

"We're being practical."

"I didn't know you were a pessimist," Donovan said, grinning to assure her he meant the comment in jest.

"Nuclear Armageddon has a way of altering a person's perspective."

Donovan saw the profound sadness mirrored in her eyes and wished he could say something witty to derail her train of thought. He was relieved when an interruption arrived in the person of his executive officer. "Yes, Mr. Percy?"

"I wanted to check on whether you'll want a Walther mounted on deck when we go through the canal."

"You're getting a little ahead of yourself, aren't you? We've got thousands of miles to cover before reaching Panama."

"With your brother back on Espiritu, I'm in charge of the gunnery detail. If we're going to use a Walther, I want to have it stripped and cleaned first, Captain."

"Clean away," Donovan said, secretly amused by the request. Before Charlie was made Chief Gunnery Officer, Percy handled such responsibilities. Donovan knew the firebrand harbored a bit of professional jealousy and suspected that cleaning the Walther had more to do with demonstrating Percy's efficiency than any urgent need to remove a few spots of dust.

Communications Officer Jennings suddenly made a startling announcement. "Captain, we're picking up a signal."

"What kind of signal?"

The answer sent an invisible electric shock through every crew member on the bridge.

"An SOS."

Charlie halted, the Franchi in his left hand, and surveyed the dense vegetation on all sides. "Are you sure he went this way?"

"I'm sure, sir," Seaman Richards responded.

"All of us saw him," Wayne added.

"Then where the hell is he?" Charlie grumbled. They were over three hundred yards into the jungle, surrounded by frolicking monkeys and singing birds. They'd raced in pursuit of Baltimore Jack to prevent the wrestler from returning to his house, but had seen no sign of the huge hermit. "He didn't just up and disappear."

"Maybe the man-eaters got him," Kent speculated.

"We couldn't be that lucky," Richards joked.

Confused, Charlie turned every which way. There were no trails, nothing to indicate the direction the giant took. "Spread out at ten-yard intervals. Always stay in sight of the men on your flanks. If you see anything, give a yell."

The detail complied, with two men going on either side of Charlie. He waited until they were strung out in a line before giving the hand signal to advance while listening to the wildlife sounds. Since Jack didn't carry weapons, he doubted the recluse would try anything stupid, but the man was unpredictable.

They traveled twenty more yards when something moved in the trees ahead.

Instantly Charlie halted and motioned for the others to

do likewise. He saw the figure draw nearer and recognized the distinctive build even though the man's features were obscured by leaves. "Baltimore Jack."

The men started to close in.

A moment later the wrestler stepped into the open and halted, regarding them without any trace of malice. "What are you guys doing out here?"

"Three guesses, and the first two don't count," Charlie snapped, walking forward.

Jack's forehead creased, then he broke into a grin. "You came after me?"

"You were told to stay in the village," Charlie said, wondering if the man was putting on an act.

"You figured I was heading home?" Jack responded, and laughed heartily.

"What's so funny?"

"You dudes are getting carried away."

"We have a job to do, mister."

Jack laughed harder, genuinely amused, his brawny hands resting on his broad hips.

Peeved, struggling to control his anger, Charlie halted a yard from the smirking giant. "I fail to see the humor in this situation."

"You would if you were in my shoes."

"Were you on your way home or not?"

"Nope," Jack said, chuckling as he watched Charlie's detail approach.

"Then what the hell are you doing way out here?"

"Nature called."

"What?"

"I don't know any of the colonists well enough to impose on them, and no one has gotten around to building public facilities," Jack explained in a condescending manner.

Charlie glanced at his companions, who were covering the giant with their Franchis, and back at Jack. "You came out this far just to take a dump?"

"I like my privacy."

Was it possible the man was telling the truth? Charlie mused, his suspicions aroused. Sure, Jack could have waltzed off to relieve himself. Then again, the man might have been watching his back trail, seen the detail in pursuit, and decided to return peacefully, concocting this story to protect his butt.

"Don't you believe me?" Jack asked.

"Does it matter?" Charlie rejoined, gesturing for the others to lower their weapons.

"You know, I don't think I like your attitude."

"I don't give a damn what you like," Charlie said, not caring if he antagonized the troublemaker. To his surprise, the wrestler grinned.

"You've got balls, Donovan. I'll give you that. Not many men have the guts to stand up to me. Must run in your family."

A compliment? Charlie pivoted, confused, and nodded in the direction of the village. "We'll escort you back."

"That'd be a mistake."

Charlie wheeled. "You can walk back under your own power or we can carry you. But one way or the other, you're going."

"You do enjoy posturing, don't you?"

"What are you talking about?"

Seaman Richards coughed. "No bricks whatsoever," he interjected.

Now it was the wrestler's turn to be puzzled. He looked at the crewman. "What are *you* talking about?"

"Nothing," Richards said lamely.

"Let's just head back, shall we?" Charlie proposed.

"And what about the bones?" Baltimore Jack asked.

"Bones?" Charlie repeated.

Jack jerked his right thumb at the vegetation behind

him. "Yeah. I stumbled on them when I was going to the bathroom. A whole pile. I'm no expert, but I'd say they're all human."

"A pile of human bones?"

"Do you want to see for yourself or stand here repeating everything I say?"

"Show us," Charlie directed. From the expressions worn by his men, they were equally mystified. He followed the giant into the trees, batting a few dangling vines aside, and then pushed through a particularly dense thicket. Jack abruptly stopped, blocking his view, and he stepped to the left, his eyes widening in astonishment.

The pile was more like a six-foot-high mound situated in the center of an overgrown clearing. There were hundreds—possibly thousands—of bones: skulls, ribs, clavicles, femurs, tibias, hipbones, and a jumbled mass of indistinguishable lesser bones. Lying around the mound were scores more, most having been cracked open and gnawed down to the marrow.

"Good God!" Seaman Parker blurted.

"What the hell is this?" Kent wanted to know.

"I have no idea," Charlie said, walking up to the mound. He placed his hand on the pile and felt the rough outer texture of a femur. From the grayish, pitted appearance, he judged the bones had been there a long, long time.

"Sure blew my mind when I saw it," Baltimore Jack mentioned. "Too bad Alex isn't here. She might know why the natives did this."

Charlie nodded absently. Alex knew more about the history and cultures of the South Pacific natives than anyone else on the island. When the colonists first arrived, it was Alex who identified the stone platform they found in the village as a *marae*, an altar used for human sacrifice. She'd estimated the *marae* had stood for centuries and voiced the optimistic opinion it hadn't been used in decades. No one felt comfortable with the thing in their midst, and Tom later had the altar removed and the micronuke erected on the exact spot.

Seaman Richards knelt and examined a gnawed radius. "I'd say these teeth marks were made recently."

"The man-eaters again?" Wayne said.

"Who knows?" Charlie said with a shrug, scanning the thick vegetation ringing the mound. From even a few yards away the site would be practically invisible. It was no wonder no one had found the bones until now.

"Should we bury them?" Parker asked.

"Why bother?" Charlie responded.

"What if some of the kids find out? They could come out here and start breaking the bones to bits. Doesn't strike me as right. For all we know, this is a native burial ground."

"Maybe," Charlie said. "But we're not doing anything until Alex returns. In the meantime, all of us will keep our traps shut. Understood?"

Everyone agreed to keep quiet with a notable exception.

"What about you, Samson?" Charlie inquired of the wrestler.

"You don't have to worry on my account. Few of the colonists bother to talk to me."

"I wonder why."

"I've wondered the same thing. I mean, I used to be the idol of millions and now I'm treated like a nobody."

"Did you ever stop to think the fact that you intimidate the hell out of everyone might be the reason?"

Baltimore Jack snorted. "I don't go around intimidating people."

"Oh, yeah? Have you taken a good look in a mirror lately?" Charlie replied, and turned. "Let's head back and check on the progress of the fence. We have a lot to do before nightfall if we want to be ready for those things."

"Hey, Donovan," Jack said. "Does everybody really find me intimidating?"

"No more so than King Kong."

"But I'm basically a mellow, decent sort of dude. I want everyone to like me."

"Then get off your high horse and quit trying to lord it over the colonists. Maybe you do own Espiritu. Maybe you don't. It doesn't matter. You don't have the right to waltz around like you're the lord and master of the island and the rest of us are just peons."

"Do I give that impression?"

"Only whenever you open your mouth," Charlie said, and took two more strides before a heavy hand fell on his right shoulder. He tensed and halted, expecting to be lifted into the air and tossed half a mile. Instead, when he shifted he saw the giant smiling.

"No one has ever talked to me the way you do," Jack stated.

"I tell it like I see it."

"I know. And I want to thank you. I'll give some thought to what you've told me."

"Whatever you think is best," Charlie said, and almost winced as the wrestler's thick fingers tightened affectionately.

Jack nodded and let go. "I like you, Donovan. You've got spunk."

Lucky me! Charlie thought, and gingerly rubbed his shoulder. He resumed hiking toward the village, grateful to have one problem alleviated. Tonight would come the real challenge.

The man-eaters would be on the prowl.

* * *

Donovan stood on the topside bridge with Alex at his side, Hooper at the helm, Executive Officer Percy to his left, and two armed crewmen behind him, his gaze riveted to the ocean northeast of their position.

"The target should be visible any second," Percy announced.

"I hope we find whoever it is alive," Alex said.

"So do I," Donovan agreed, raising binoculars to his eyes, "but I'm not very optimistic. The signal is weak. They must be operating on battery power, and the battery is on its last legs. Don't get your hopes up."

"What a spoilsport," Alex said. "We finally get the chance to rescue another survivor, and you act as if we're going to attend a funeral."

Donovan swept the binoculars from side to side, then riveted his gaze to an unmistakable silhouette outlined on the horizon. "I see it," he informed them, adjusting the central focusing drive until the details were crystal clear.

The source of the SOS was a battered schooner eighty feet long. Both the mainmast and the foremast were broken, the sails hanging in tatters and flapping in the wind. The spars and the hull showed evidence of scorching.

"Mr. Percy, run below and get pistols and Franchis for both of us," Donovan ordered.

"On my way, Captain. Do you want a deck gun set up?"

"I see no need for a Walther. Just the sidearms and the Franchis, if you please."

Percy nodded and made for the hatch.

"I'd like to board with you," Alex said.

"No."

"You know I can handle myself."

"Once we've established it's safe, you can come over," Donovan promised. "And that reminds me." He stabbed the intercom button. "Mr. Jennings?"

"Yes, Captain?"

"Anything new?"

"No, sir. Sensors indicate elevated radioactivity but she's not hot enough to pose a risk if you don't stay more than half an hour. There are no engine noises and no heat generation. If it wasn't for the SOS, I'd say she's a dead one."

"And still no response to our message?"

"None, sir. I've tried repeatedly, but no one answers. Maybe the transmitter is on automatic."

"I've had the same thought," Donovan said. "Okay. Keep trying. And activate the recording system. I want a tape for the files."

Liberator was equipped with a system for recording digitally all information from the external sensors, which included sonar, radar, the lasers, and radio, and storing it in the Cray-9 computer. Data from scientific detectors and thermal probes could also be saved and stored. A particularly useful feature of the system was its videotape recording capability using the blister-mounted cameras to make a visual record of the sub's surroundings.

"One more thing," Donovan added. "Put it on the monitors so everyone can see."

There were monitors located at the workstations, in the living quarters, and at other strategic points throughout the sub, enabling the crew members to view whatever was fed into the system.

"Anything else, Captain?"

"No. Donovan out." He walked aft and stared down at the turtleback. Flazy and a junior officer from the engineering section were perched on the safety line track.

When Flazy glanced up, Donovan waved and motioned for them to return, then moved forward to gaze at the distant schooner.

"Having any second thoughts about leaving Espiritu?" Alex asked.

The unexpected question made Donovan glance at her. "No. Why?"

"Just wondering. After your initial reservations, such a reaction would be only natural."

Donovan grinned. "You should have been a psychiatrist. I'm not preoccupied with worry about Charlie and the colonists, if that's what you're getting at. I have complete confidence in him."

"Of course you do. He's a Donovan."

"Meaning?"

"If he wanted to go on the schooner, you'd let him."

"Ah," Donovan said, and nodded. "Now I understand. My decision to have you stay here until we ascertain if there's any danger has nothing to do with your competence. You're officially our science officer, not a small arms expert, and science officers routinely do not venture into potential combat situations. Read the regs."

"So you're just going by the book."

"What else? I'm not coddling you, Alex. I'm too damn proud of your competence to do that."

Alex looked down at her shoes. "Thanks," she said softly.

Liberator slowly neared the schooner, cruising at a steady twenty knots, spray hissing over her bow.

Donovan heard someone huffing up the ladder from the deck and rotated to see Chief Smith and the junior officer climb onto the bridge. "What's the verdict?"

Flazy took a second to take a deep breath, then reported. "Our visual inspection confirms the computer readings. There's no sign of structural damage. I'd say the hull and the keel are intact." He paused. "But we can't see the underside unless we dive down or put the ship in dry dock, and we can't be one hundred percent certain until then."

"I won't settle for anything less," Donovan said.

At that moment Percy's head popped out of the hatch. He handed a pair of Franchis to one of the crewmen, then climbed all the way out. Strapped around his waist was a Colt, and slung over his left shoulder was a brown belt with a holster on it containing a second pistol. "I have the guns you wanted, Captain," he stated.

As Donovan took the gunbelt he nodded at Flazy. "Chief Smith needs two men in diving gear to join him aft when we stop to check the schooner. He'll instruct them in what to do."

"I'll get right on it," Percy said, and stepped to the intercom.

Donovan secured the belt buckle, then grabbed a Franchi. "Take your time, Flazy," he said. "We won't move until you're completely satisfied the whale didn't cause any damage."

Flazy nodded, sighed, and moved to the ladder. "I never knew a man could get so much exercise on a sub," he remarked as he lifted his bulk over the side.

Chuckling, Donovan stood beside Alex and checked the Franchi's magazine.

"I hope you don't need to use that," she said, a tinge of apprehension in her tone.

Donovan gazed at the drifting hulk, his eyes narrowing. "You and me both."

Liberator dwarfed the sailing ship. From the top of the blister Donovan and company had an unobstructed view of part of the schooner's deck. Sections of broken masts lay tangled in fouled rigging amid strips of torn sails. Oddly, there were pieces of broken furniture, shredded clothing, busted dishes, and other items scattered about. Dark stains were visible. But there wasn't a soul in sight.

"I don't like the looks of it," Alex mentioned.

Percy grunted in assent. "Why would anyone smash all their furniture and tear up their clothes? Makes no sense."

"Let's go over and find out," Donovan suggested.

A four-man crew was already on the foredeck and had an inflatable in the water, ready to go. Nearby were two men armed with M16s, ready to respond to any threats.

Donovan repeatedly glanced at the schooner as he climbed down from the bridge. Painted in large black letters on the bow was the name *Taj Mahal*. He wondered if the vessel had been caught in a firestorm during the war. The blistering heat would account for the charred wood and the destruction to the spars and masts. If so, the likelihood of discovering any survivors was extremely remote unless the people on board had all been below when the firestorm hit.

An enormous shark fin broke the surface fifty yards

from the sub's bow, traveled for half that distance on a northerly course, then sank into the ocean again.

"Did you see that, Captain?" Percy asked.

"Yeah. Try not to fall overboard on the way over."

Percy grinned. "Don't worry. I don't intend to end my days as shark food."

One of the crewmen extended a familiar object clasped in his left hand as they approached. "Here's the radio you wanted, sir."

Donovan took the transceiver and paused to switch it on and to press the transmit button. "Mr. Jennings, do you read me?"

"Loud and clear, sir."

"You will have the conn while Mr. Percy and I are on the schooner."

"Yes, sir."

"If sensors pick up anything unusual, I don't care how minor, you're to inform me immediately."

"Will do."

"Donovan out." He clipped the transceiver to his belt and stepped down onto the starboard diving plane. A pair of seamen held the inflatable steady while he took a seat.

Executive Officer Percy had a few last words for the men armed with M16s. "Keep your eyes peeled. With Charlie and his men absent, you're the best shots on board. We'll be counting on you to cover us."

"We'll do the best we can, sir," pledged the slimmer of the duo.

"Can't ask for more," Percy said, and hopped into the inflatable.

Since only sixty feet separated the two vessels, they used oars and paddled to the schooner instead of resorting to the outboard. The air was deathly, eerily still. A faint, fetid odor clung to the schooner like an invisible garment.

"Whew!" Percy exclaimed, and sneezed. "Disgusting. We should have brought along gas masks."

Nodding, Donovan opened a compartment on the side of the inflatable and removed a grappling hook attached to forty feet of nylon rope knotted at twelve-inch intervals.

"I'll go first, sir," Percy quickly offered.

"Rank has its privileges," Donovan responded, and carefully coiled the nylon at his feet. He grasped the rope two feet below the forked hooks and swung the grapnel in a circle until the metal was a blur, then arced his right arm up and over, releasing the rope at the critical moment.

The grappling hook sailed on high and narrowly missed the gunwale. Gravity brought it down with a loud splash close to the inflatable.

"If at first you don't succeed," Donovan muttered, and repeated the procedure. This time he fared better; the hooks caught on the craft and held fast. He tugged repeatedly to ensure that the rope would support his weight. "Here goes nothing," he said, and slung the Franchi over his left shoulder.

"Watch yourself, Captain."

"You know it." Donovan started up, climbing hand over hand, his arm muscles straining, his shoulders protesting the treatment. In recent months he'd rarely had time for exercise, and when he reached the top every aching sinew in his body reminded him of the fact. He slid onto the deck, unslung the submachine gun, and motioned for Percy to join him.

Close-up the shambles on the deck and the stench were worse. Much of the debris appeared to have been arranged in haphazard piles with narrow cleared paths between them. The dark stains scattered about displayed a discomforting crimson tinge.

Blood, maybe? Donovan wondered, scrutinizing the

shattered masts and fouled rigging. There could be no doubt now about the cause. The cabin, cockpit, deck, and even the wheel also displayed the prominent exterior burn marks so characteristic of the effects of a firestorm. Apparently the boat had drifted ever since.

Donovan focused on the companionway, his nerves on edge. A troubling sensation came over him whenever he boarded one of these derelicts, a feeling of impending menace, and his skin prickled as if from a heat rash. When Percy suddenly appeared over the side, he almost jumped. "All clear," he said gruffly.

The executive officer slipped to the deck and unlimbered his Franchi. "Ready when you are, Captain," he whispered.

So much for the privileges of rank, Donovan mused as he advanced cautiously toward the doorway. With every stride the vile odor grew progressively worse.

"Smells like rotten meat," Percy commented.

Donovan didn't want to think about the possible source. He forced himself to move to the companionway and halted to listen. The steps and the passage below were murky, obscuring whatever lurked below. Placing his back against the right-hand wall, he went lightly down and paused, scarcely breathing. The stench was terrible. Waiting until his eyes adjusted to the gloom, he inched forward.

Percy did the same along the opposite wall.

They covered five yards before a doorway materialized on the right.

Tightening his grip on the Franchi, Donovan peered around the jamb to discover the galley. He distinguished the sink, stove, and an icebox. There was no table, no chairs, and he guessed they were topside, smashed to pieces. Gesturing with his left arm, he led the way deeper into the boat. The smell prompted him to place his left palm over his mouth and nose.

Soon they came to the salon, where sunlight streamed in from a pair of ports to reveal a scene from someone's worst nightmare.

"My God," Percy declared in horror.

There were six corpses arranged bizarrely around the cabin. All had been stripped naked. All were rotted beyond recognition, their bones exposed in spots, ribbons of flesh hanging from their bodies. Two were seated on the settee, one was sprawled on top of the dinette table, and three lay on the floor, their arms neatly aligned at their sides, their grisly, ragged lips pulled back to expose their yellowing teeth in ghastly grins of welcome.

Percy had his right hand over his mouth. "What gives? Did they just sit down and die? Who took off their clothes?"

Instead of replying, which would entail opening his mouth and inhaling more of the stench, Donovan simply shrugged. His stomach churned and threatened to erupt, and he swallowed bitter bile. Quickly he stepped over the corpses barring the passage and hurried forward to the stateroom. A sight he would never forget greeted his appalled gaze.

All the furniture except a single chair and table had been removed. On the table rested a sophisticated shortwave set, a Higachi 2007, one of the last models manufactured before the war. A flickering red light indicated the unit was on the verge of expending the last of its battery power.

At the chair sat a man clothed in a peculiar, shiny white suit that shimmered in the golden rays pouring through a nearby port. He had not been dead long enough for his flesh to putrefy, but his skin appeared to have shrunk so that the bones underneath were visible. More than anything else, he resembled a well-dressed skeleton. His shoulders were slumped, his chin sagged on his chest, and a gaping hole in his left temple served as a counterpoint for a smaller hole on the right. Clutched in the rigid fingers of his right hand was a revolver.

"A suicide," Percy commented.

Donovan walked closer, puzzled by the satiny sheen to the suit. The material was unlike any he knew, and he didn't understand the reason until he glanced down and spied a can of white spray paint lying under the chair.

Percy also noticed. "Did he paint his clothes?"

"Looks that way."

"What a loony."

"Radiation psychosis produces strange behavior."

Nodding absently, Percy glanced back toward the salon. "This guy must have been the last to kick. He probably set up those others, then came in here and blew his brains out."

"See if you can find any flammable liquid," Donovan directed. "If not, grab clothes, towels, sheets, anything that will burn readily and make a pile near the companionway."

"We're going to set the whole boat on fire, Captain?"

"We can't very well bury them, can we?"

Percy sheepishly shook his head and hastened off.

Unclipping the transceiver, Donovan raised it to his lips. "Mr. Jennings, do you copy?"

"Five-by, sir."

"There are no survivors. Repeat, no survivors. Inform Dr. Fisher his services won't be needed. Mr. Percy and I are going to set the boat ablaze, then head back."

"What about the SOS?"

Frowning, Donovan reached out and pressed on a silver toggle switch below the blinking red light, shutting off the power. The light and all the dials went dead. "Just like you figured. Their radio was set on automatic."

"Sorry to hear that, Captain."

"No sorrier than I am. Donovan out." He lowered the transceiver and was about to depart when his eyes fell on a small notebook under the man's left arm. On the assumption it was a log or journal and of possible interest, he gingerly grabbed the man's forearm and slowly lifted. Flakes of paint peeled under his grip, and the arm felt as light as the proverbial feather. He slid the brown notebook out and placed it in a pocket for later study. With a final glance at the stately corpse, he exited the stateroom and rejoined Percy, who was in the act of adding an armful of linens to a pile of towels already lying in the middle of the passageway.

"The only flammable liquid I've found so far is a can of kerosene about a third full," the executive officer reported. "It's in a cabinet in the galley."

"That will do nicely."

In ten minutes they heaped together a chest-high mound of fabrics and materials. Percy poured the kerosene over the top and sides and tossed the can aside.

Donovan had to feel each of his pockets before he found his lighter in his shirt. Weeks ago he'd smoked the last of his cigarettes, but he still carried the engraved silver lighter, a gift from his father, out of force of habit. He had to flick it four times before it sparked and flamed. Leaning forward, he ignited the pile, then whirled and dashed up the steps to the deck.

He let Percy go down the rope first, and by the time he gripped the nylon and started over the gunwale great clouds of smoke billowed from the companionway. Fingers of red and orange licked at the edge of the cabin and a rosy light lit up the ports.

Descending was ridiculously easy. As soon as his feet touched, he whipped the nylon from side to side and front to back until the grappling hook loosened and plummeted into the sea. Reeling in the rope took no time at all, and soon they were paddling toward *Liberator*.

Once they were clear of the stench, Donovan inhaled gratefully, cleaning out his lungs. He saw Alex wave and lifted his arm to return the gesture when one of the crewmen on the foredeck pointed to the west and shouted an urgent warning.

"Captain, look out! A shark! A shark!"

Twisting, Donovan spied an enormous fin, probably the same one they'd seen earlier, knifing the water as the beast hurtled directly toward the inflatable. The voracious killer must have circled the sub, seeking prey.

The men with the M16s opened fire, their rounds stitching the surface near the fin with no apparent effect.

"It might try to capsize us," Percy declared, standing. He aimed carefully and fired, the blasting of his Franchi drowning out the M16s.

Donovan swept erect, leveled his submachine gun, but held his fire, waiting for the right moment. Despite the hail of lead, the shark came on rapidly, its upper back and head visible just below the surface. Only thirty yards separated the bobbing inflatable from the massive, living engine of destruction when the M16s and Percy's Franchi went empty.

Which was Donovan's cue to cut loose. He remembered the lessons his brother had given and trained the barrel a few feet in front of the shark before stroking the trigger, the marginal recoil bucking the gun slightly, then tracked his firing pattern to concentrate on the shark's head and eyes. His shots scored. He could see them smacking into the animal's tough hide. But still the eating machine came on.

Percy slapped in a new magazine and added his firepower.

Both crewmen were also pouring rounds into the animal's side.

Suddenly the shark veered toward the schooner, then abruptly dived, blood trailing in its wake, to disappear in the murky realm below.

"Quickly! We must get to the ship before more show up," Donovan directed, and dropped to his knees to paddle furiously.

"Or that one comes back," Percy added, and applied himself to his paddle with equal enthusiasm.

The four-man retrieval crew was ready and waiting to grab the inflatable the instant it touched. They held the raft steady so the officers could jump out.

"Look behind you, Captain," one of them said.

Donovan turned and frowned. Already two smaller fins were crisscrossing the space between the vessels. A third popped up a second later.

"That was too close for comfort," Percy commented.

Nodding, Donovan gazed at the schooner. Flames were dancing above the cabin and smoke shrouded the deck. Soon the vessel would be an inferno. Since there was no reason to stick around and watch it burn, he walked toward the blister. "Let's get under way."

"Do you think Flazy and the divers are done inspecting the hull?"

The divers! Donovan had forgotten about them in the excitement of the shark attack. He raced to the ladder and climbed to the topside bridge.

Alex took one look at his face and asked, "What's the matter?"

Donovan dashed past her and looked down, relieved to see the chief engineer, the junior officer, and two dripping divers staring at the sharks. He cupped his hands to his mouth and shouted, "Did you find anything?"

Flazy yelled back, "The ship is A-OK, Captain. No damage whatsoever."

"Good. Get below. We're heading for the Panama Canal."

A broad grin creased the engineer's fleshy features. "Any chance of doing a little swimming first?"

"If you want my opinion, sir," Seaman Richards remarked, "that fence wouldn't keep out a herd of rampaging rabbits."

Charlie glanced at the bearded crewman. "You must read a lot of science fiction."

The statement surprised Richards. "I'm a big science fiction fan. How did you know?"

"I took a wild guess," Charlie said, and gestured at the object of their conversation. "And I know this won't keep the man-eaters out. There wasn't time to construct a proper palisade, so we compromised and settled for an early warning system."

"Let's hope a strong wind doesn't come up," Richards said.

Ignoring the crack, Charlie stepped up to the completed fence and gazed in both directions. Despite the time constraint and the limited building supplies, the colonists had done a rustic but fine job of erecting an initial line of defense against the mysterious nocturnal killers.

Four feet high and tilted outward at a forty-five-degree angle, the fence consisted of a variety of boards and limbs nailed together in roughly uniform order. Firmly secured at two-foot intervals and jutting outward from the top an additional six inches were sharpened branches designed to impale anything trying to get in. As an added precaution, tin cans, pots, pans, and other noisemakers dangled from wires strung at regular intervals.

"This will do the job nicely," Charlie said, and tilted his head to stare at the fantastic celestial display overhead. Stars literally filled the firmament. Whether because of the island's location or the fact that there were no bright city lights to cast an interfering glare in the atmosphere, he could see more stars than he'd ever witnessed from any other place he'd ever been.

He turned and surveyed the rows of huts, thinking of all the slumbering colonists snug in their beds. At two in the morning the majority of them were in dreamland; only a few windows were illuminated by candles or lanterns burning within.

"What if these things don't show up tonight?" Richards asked.

"Then we keep watch tomorrow night and every night until they do."

"I take it we're supposed to sleep during the day."

"Sleep? What's that?" Charlie joked, and adjusted the Franchi slung over his left shoulder. He nodded at Richards and started north along the perimeter. "I'd best be continuing on my rounds. Remember, give a yell if you see anything."

Richards tapped the transceiver attached to his belt. "You'll be the first to know, sir."

A cool breeze softly stroked Charlie's face as he walked. He'd distributed his men at the four points of the compass; Richards just inside the fence to the west of the village, Wayne to the north, Parker to the east, and Kent to the south. And with him acting as a rover, there was little likelihood of the animals getting among the huts undetected.

He switched his attention to the murky tract of tangled vegetation beyond the fence. Initially he'd contemplated perching his men in trees at the edge of the jungle where they would have a better view and a clear field of fire, but he'd changed his mind after realizing they would be unable to adequately protect the colonists should the beasts enter the village and try to break into the huts. Such a possibility was a slim one, but he had to weigh every scenario and compensate accordingly.

Charlie took several more strides when his transceiver crackled softly and Wayne's voice whispered urgently, "Post One reporting. I have something here."

He lifted the radio to his lips. "Charlie here. What have you got?"

"Something is moving in the undergrowth, sir."

"Can you be more specific?"

"Nope. All I hear is the snapping of twigs and the rattling of bushes. I can't see what's making the noise."

"On my way," Charlie said, and unslung the Franchi with one hand as he ran. He stayed close to the fence, his eyes probing the inky foliage, hoping for a glimpse of the man-eaters.

Seaman Wayne materialized up ahead, crouched in the open space between the fence and the huts, his submachine gun leveled. He glanced around at the sound of Charlie's footsteps and motioned frantically for Charlie to hurry.

Nothing moved under the trees.

"I don't hear them now," Wayne announced in a whisper.

"Do you think there was more than one?"

"There had to be from all the noise they were making."

Kneeling beside the crewman, Charlie listened expectantly but heard only the breeze stirring the leaves. He wondered if the young seaman was suffering from a case of the jitters. Granted, there must have been *something* out there, but the man-eaters invariably exercised supreme stealth and there was no reason to think the things would suddenly change their pattern of behavior.

"I know I heard them, sir," Wayne stated.

"I believe you," Charlie said.

They waited in silence for several minutes with no result. If there were any animals abroad they were being deathly quiet.

"It figures," Wayne muttered. "Now you'll think I made the whole thing up."

"No I won't."

"They were there, I tell you."

"Maybe I scared them off when I ran up," Charlie suggested. "Keep your eyes peeled. They might come back." He stood and gazed along the fence.

Abruptly, from off in the distance arose a mournful, protracted, wavering howl. Distorted by the wind and the trees, the wail possessed an eery, almost demonic quality. It lingered on and on, gradually tapering off to a low whine.

Charlie felt goose bumps erupt all over his flesh. The howls were enough to make a person start believing in werewolves. He knew the sounds came from the northwest, from near the volcano, where most of the howling was heard. In some way he couldn't fathom, the volcano must be the key to the mystery.

"Too bad we don't have any land mines," Seaman Wayne remarked. "I'd feel more comfortable with a mine field between me and those things than this flimsy fence."

"Why is everyone picking on the poor fence?" Charlie responded, and resumed his perimeter check, looking back at the nervous Wayne. "Hang in there. If you hear anything else, don't hesitate to call me."

"I won't make a fool of myself again."

"Better safe than sorry," Charlie said, and felt compelled to add, "And that's an order, mister."

"Yes, sir."

He faced front and walked toward Parker's post, preoccupied with the dilemma, and pondered whether there might be a way to trap the beasts. Cages were out of the question; the things would smell the human scent and not come anywhere near them. Snares wouldn't work, either. Any animal large enough to take down a man in a matter of seconds was too big to be strangled by a simple wire snare. He sighed and said to himself, "Where's an Indian when you need one?"

"India?"

The unexpected reply startled Charlie and he swung around to face the huts, bringing the Franchi up. A massive form stood in the dark space between two dwellings. "Who the hell?" he blurted.

"Sorry, dude. Didn't mean to scare you," declared Baltimore Jack as he came closer, grinning impishly.

"You didn't scare me," Charlie snapped, jerking the submachine gun down. "But you damn near had your fool head blown off. What the hell are you doing out here at this time of night?"

"I couldn't sleep," the wrestler said, and stretched, his huge muscles bulging. "Probably because I'm supposed to crash out on a sleeping bag in a house belonging to someone I hardly know. If I was in my own bed, I'd be sleeping like a baby."

"Now don't start with that again," Charlie said gruffly.

"I'm not going to give you a hard time," Jack stated. "I'm just stating facts. The Gordons are nice folks and all, and I appreciate they had the decency to invite me to stay with them, but it's not the same as home. You know what I mean?"

"I guess I do," Charlie admitted, resuming his patrol. "Well, I've got work to do. Catch you later. Don't stray past the fence."

"Mind if I tag along?"

Charlie almost told the giant, tactfully of course, to get lost. But the man was only trying to be friendly.

For some strange reason, the wrestler seemed to regard him as a potential pal. It figured. He always did have a knack for attracting the weirdos. Memories of Boston, of the tattooed belly dancer and her one-eyed cat, made him shudder.

"What about it, dude?" Baltimore Jack prodded.

"Tag along if you want. But keep the noise down."

"I'll be as quiet as a mouse, little buddy."

"My name's not Gilligan."

"What?" Jack said, and then burst into hearty laughter. "Gilligan! I get it. That's a good one."

"Shhhhhh," Charlie hissed, his finger over his lips. "Not so loud, dummy." No sooner had the last word left his lips than he realized his mistake and braced for a sock on the jaw. Surprisingly, the wrestler only chuckled.

"Sorry, dude. But you've got a great sense of humor."

Charlie glanced at the giant's face to see if he was being sarcastic. He wasn't.

"Actually," Jack went on, "I was hoping to bump into you."

"You were?"

"Yeah. I've been thinking about everything you said earlier today, about me intimidating folks, and I came to the conclusion you're right. Inadvertently I have been."

"What do you plan to do about it?"

"Stop."

Not knowing quite what to say and puzzled that the wrestler chose to bare his soul to him, Charlie mentioned the first thing that came into his head. "Takes a big man to admit when he's wrong."

For a few moments they walked in silence.

"Do you know what happened today?" Baltimore Jack asked, and went on before Charlie could answer. "I'll tell you. I was walking through the village this evening, just strolling around to check out all the improvements the colonists have made, and I saw this little boy point at me and say to his sister, 'There goes the mean man.' Imagine that! A kid calling me mean."

"Hit you hard, did it?"

"You don't know the half of it. I mean, I used to bounce kids on my knees at my autograph-signing sessions. Hundreds of thousands of them sent in for my T-shirts, videos, and toys. I was their hero. Now I'm an ogre."

"My grandfather used to have a favorite saying that stuck in my mind when I was growing up. It pretty well describes your situation."

"What is it?"

"We get what we deserve."

"Ouch."

"Sorry."

"Don't be. You're right on the money." Baltimore Jack smiled and clapped Charlie on the back. "I like you. I hope the two of us can become friends."

"If you loosen up I'll bet you make a lot of friends."

"I hope so. If more people had your spunk, I might have come to my senses long ago."

Charlie spied Seaman Parker standing near the fence and waved.

"There's something I don't understand, though," Jack said.

"What?"

"You're such a decent guy. What the hell happened to your brother?"

Donovan was on his back in bed, his head propped on his left hand, staring at the ceiling. Alex nestled beside him, her breathing regular, her breasts rising and falling with the rhythm of her sleep. He idly stroked her hair, reviewing the day's events, unable to shake the haunting image of the man in the painted suit.

What a horrible way to go, he reflected, and thought of all the millions who had died ghastly deaths during and just after the war. Many more would undoubtedly perish in the months ahead, most notably those who suffered from radiation poisoning yet tenaciously clung to life. The dreaded white-shirts were a prime example. They were walking ghouls, their bodies ravaged, their minds seemingly gone, but somehow they continued to function on a primitive, bestial level.

He wished Pete Fisher would discover the cause of the disease soon. Knowing that radiation was to blame wasn't enough. *How* did the radiation induce the psychosis? What changes were effected in the human metabolism? Why did those so afflicted always wear white? There were so many questions and not enough answers.

He worried about another aspect. What if the disease was transmitted by breathing contaminated air? What was the danger to his crew if they passed through an infected zone? Was he taking an extreme risk by sailing to New York? After all, the health and safety of the crew came first. Why expose all of them to rescue two families?

Donovan felt Alex stir and mumble incoherently. Her hand moved, her fingers running lightly up his chest to his chin, then over his mouth and nose to his forehead, lingering at the sides of his eyes.

"What are you doing awake, lover?"

"Couldn't sleep."

"Obviously," Alex said huskily, tracing a fingernail across his brow. "What's bothering you? Are you still upset because we can't raise Ronca and Hardesty?"

"They should have answered by now."

"Maybe their batteries ran low."

"Pete assured me they'd scavenged enough to last a couple of years."

Alex placed her forearm on his chest and rested her chin on top, her eyes lovingly scrutinizing his dim features.

"There are any number of reasons why they haven't contacted us. Why worry until you have something concrete to worry about?"

"I like to do all my worrying in advance. That way I'm prepared for the worst."

"How many days before we reach New York?"

"Five if we push it and have no problems. Realistically, more like seven."

"If you worry that long you'll wind up with an ulcer," Alex joked.

"An ulcer would be preferable to radiation insanity."

"What?"

Donovan looped his right arm around her shoulders. "I've been lying here thinking—"

"Uh-oh."

"—and wondering if there's a possibility all of us might develop the psychosis."

"So that's it." Alex gazed at the bulkhead and her voice lowered. "Pete and I have examined the same possibility. We ran a number of tests on ourselves and put the computer through its paces."

"And?"

"And we really don't know. Our tests and the checkups we've been running on the colonists show everyone is healthy. We've detected no abnormalities in their blood, nothing in the respiratory tracts or the digestive systems of anyone on Espiritu that would indicate the presence of an unknown virus or bacteria."

"Maybe you'd need to examine a live white-shirt to learn the answer."

"For all we know they might be contagious."

Donovan sat up so quickly she slid down into his lap. "Damn. I never thought of that. And we fought them in San Francisco. We were right next to them, breathing the same air they did. I even touched one of the things." He shuddered, recalling the charging male white-shirt he'd punched in the mouth. The single blow had crushed the man's face like an overripe melon, leaving blood, flesh, and an oily substance clinging to his fingers and knuckles.

"Calm down, lover," Alex said, sitting beside him. She ran her hand through his hair and tenderly kissed him on the cheek. "Pete has given us a clean bill of health."

"What if there is an incubation period?" Donovan mused aloud.

"If there is, there's nothing we can do about it right now. Just count your blessings and quit being so morbid."

"Sorry. I guess seeing those corpses on the schooner rattled me more than I knew."

"You need something to take your mind off them."

"Oh. Like what?"

Alex grinned, put her arms on his thighs, and leaned closer until their lips almost touched. "Since we're both up anyway, why don't we make the most of it?"

"Anyone ever tell you that you have a one-track mind?"

"Are you complaining?"

Donovan smiled. "Nope. Counting my blessings." He took her in his arms, their mouths and bodies fusing as one, and together they sank onto the sheet.

12

The third day of their voyage.

Donovan sat in his swivel chair on the bridge and studied the dazzling holographic display. *Liberator* was approaching the Panama Canal in the middle of the inbound shipping channel, moving at only twenty-five knots. He didn't want a repeat of their last visit to the Canal Zone, when the surging current caught them in its grip and shot them into the canal like a rocket. "Are the channel markers still in place, Mr. Jennings?" he asked, referring to the laser channel markers installed by the Corps of Engineers after the outbreak of the Central American War. The same type of markers had served to guide ships into American ports for years by enabling the vessels to follow a clearly defined computer track, minimizing the risk of collisions and subsequent damage to the environment.

"They're still there, Captain. Active radar shows no change in the shore features since the ship's last visit."

"What do you read on the current?"

"Less than one knot."

"The last time it was three to five knots out this far and over fifteen in the canal," Donovan mentioned thoughtfully. "Since the current has stabilized, it's a safe bet our nuking operation was successful. But I'm taking no chances. Mr. Hooper, slow to twenty knots."

"Aye, Captain."

Drumming his fingers on the chair arms, Donovan watched the three-dimensional depiction of the horizon's outline widen and clarify on the screen.

"We have readings on the canal entrance," Jennings announced. "Still five miles wide there but it's now four miles wide five miles inland and a mile and a half across starting eight miles in."

"Then it's widened since before," Donovan said.

"Nuking the east end must have created a massive suction effect, just like the computer said it would," Executive Officer Percy commented. "Water from the Pacific poured into the canal and caused more massive erosion all the way to the Atlantic."

Donovan remembered the white-shirts camped on the north side, hundreds of them seeking vainly to cross into South America, and hoped the flooding waters had put an end to their demented lives. "What's the current in the canal?"

"Current reads one to three knots," Jennings replied.

"Okay. Mr. Hooper, take us in. Stay in the center of the deep channel carved out by the current."

"Yes, sir."

"Mr. Jennings, what about clearance under the keel?"

"Plenty of room, Captain. We're at seventy feet now and there's another two hundred feet under us."

"Good. What does sonar tell us about obstructions?"

"None to speak of. The current has swept most everything away. I know the canal had chronic trouble with landslides before the war, but that was when it was only a hundred and ten feet wide. We don't have to worry about them now."

"That's for damn sure," Donovan agreed.

Liberator cruised gracefully into the center of the canal, in stark contrast to their previous entrance, when she had been buffeted ruthlessly.

"Bring us to periscope depth, Mr. Hooper."

"Periscope depth it is, sir."

Donovan sensed rather than heard someone step next to his chair and turned to find his ladylove. "You're just in time. We're going to try and reach the Atlantic."

"Think you will this time?" Alex asked, her eyes on Cyclops.

"Too soon to tell. We won't know for certain until we see whether our missile totally obliterated the barrier at the east end of the canal. But it looks promising." Donovan paused. "What have you been up to?"

"What else? Working with Pete on the psychosis."

"Any results?"

Alex frowned. "I wish."

"We're at periscope depth, Captain," Hooper interrupted.

"Up 'scope," Donovan directed, and left his chair to scan both shores and the waterway ahead. He already knew from his previous visit that the surrounding terrain had been largely obliterated and nothing much remained of the old countryside. Stark, charred spires were all that remained of Panama City. The Miraflores and Pedro Miguel locks no longer existed, and the Gaillard Cut now resembled a strait. Most of the landslide problem for the former canal had been in the cut, where as much as 1,000,000 cubic yards of loose earth were removed annually.

Shortly they came to Gatun Lake, once an artificially created 22-mile channel and now so huge that it was impossible to see any shore from the middle. There was no sign of the water hyacinths that had once plagued shipping in the lake. Many a vessel had its propellers entangled in the long, coarse roots of the prolific aquatic plant with the violet-colored flowers, and close to 50,000 of the hyacinths had been destroyed every year in an attempt to keep the waterway clear.

"We're reading a few channel markers on the bottom," Jennings disclosed.

"Any sign of the whirlpool we encountered last trip?" Donovan inquired.

"None, Captain."

The signs were more encouraging by the minute, Donovan reflected.

"All the islands that were in the lake are now submerged," Jennings reported. "They don't pose a threat to us."

"Hey, Captain," Percy interjected. "Do you want to check out Ciudad Romanus?"

On the south side of Gatun Lake had once existed the old port of Frijoles, later torn down so that Ciudad Romanus could be built in its place. Constructed by the Panamanian dictator of the same name, and designed to be radiation-proof and blastproof, Ciudad Romanus had survived the nuclear detonation relatively intact. On their previous mission here the crew had wound up embroiled in a private war between the dictator and Colombian drug lords.

"No," Donovan answered. "We're not going to let ourselves be sidetracked again. This time we go straight through to New York." He rotated the periscope to the northwest, searching for evidence of the mammoth wall of earth and sand that once blocked passage through the canal. All he found was another strait. "It looks like clear sailing the rest of the way."

"The Gatun Locks are gone," Jennings said. "And I'm not reading any channel markers."

"Any obstructions on this side of the lake?"

"No, sir."

"Getting better and better," Donovan said, and stepped back. "Down 'scope." He waited until the order was obeyed before issuing another. "Surface, Mr. Hooper."

"Aye, Captain."

"Mr. Jennings, I will be going topside with Mr. Percy and our science officer. You will keep me posted of any developments."

"Of course," Jennings replied, his tone betraying a hint

of annoyance that his competence should be doubted.

"I just don't want a repeat of the whale incident," Donovan explained, and looked at Alex. "Care for some fresh air?"

The bright sun caused all three of them to squint.

Donovan pressed binoculars to his eyes and surveyed the banks on both sides, where the lush jungle came right down to the water's edge. He thought of the jaguar attacks they'd had to contend with before and felt glad they were not setting foot off the submarine.

Their passage through the strait proved uneventful. Donovan swung to the east and spied Colon, the second largest city in Panama prior to the war, or what was left of it. A few tall buildings still stood, but even at a distance he detected their shattered glass and scorched exteriors.

"At least we can get through the canal without any problem," Percy commented as the ship headed out across the Caribbean Sea.

Alex nodded. "Now we can explore the Atlantic Seaboard. Europe. Africa."

"One step at a time, Marco Polo," Donovan quipped. "First we rescue Ronca and Hardesty."

"You don't want to stop off in Havana and pick up some cigars?"

"Are you kidding? I'm finally off cigarettes after all these years. Why tempt my willpower with another nasty habit?"

Alex chuckled. "What willpower? The only reason you quit smoking was because you ran out of cigarettes and so did everyone else. You can't even bum a smoke if you want."

"Rub it in."

"If you don't mind my saying so, sir," Percy said, "I'm glad you've stopped. I never liked breathing in all that smoke. There were scientific studies conducted that proved just standing next to a smoker could be hazardous to a person's health."

Donovan glanced from one to the other. "What is this, a conspiracy? I know about the studies, which is why I tried to confine my smoking to areas where there weren't many others around. And since I've stopped, this whole discussion is moot."

"My, my. Aren't we touchy," Alex said with a grin.

Sighing, Donovan scanned the horizon and pondered which course to take. They could travel northwest and go through the Yucatan Channel into the Gulf of Mexico and then swing east through the Straits of Florida to the Atlantic, or they could head northeast now across the Caribbean Sea to the strait between the Dominican Republic and Puerto Rico and turn due north then. He opted for the first course. They would be closer to land and better able to monitor weak SOS signals, if any. And he wanted a look at Cuba and the Florida coastline. He stabbed the intercom. "Mr. Hooper."

"Yes, sir?" the nineteen-year-old responded dutifully.

"Lay in a course for the Yucatan Channel. Thirty knots, if you please."

"Aye, Skipper."

Donovan released the button and heard a snicker.

"Changed your mind about a cigar, huh?" Alex baited him.

"Shouldn't you be testing the atmosphere or something?"

"Already done. Radiation minimal."

"My, my," Donovan said, mimicking her earlier statement. "Aren't we becoming efficient in our old age."

"That crack will cost you, lover," Alex joked, then caught herself and glanced sheepishly at Percy. She and Donovan had made an agreement not to flaunt their relationship in front of the crew and she'd done just that.

The executive officer had developed an inordinate

interest in the Panamanian coastline.

To cover her slight embarrassment Alex leaned on the rail and said to no one in particular, "Isn't it exciting to be heading for the eastern U.S.? Who knows what we'll find? Maybe a lot more survivors."

"We can only hope," Donovan said while staring through the binoculars.

"If Ronca and Hardesty survived, there must be others," Alex said.

Percy turned. "Then why haven't we heard from them? If there are more survivors, surely they can scavenge a radio and broadcast an SOS? But we've heard nothing." He paused. "For that matter we should have heard broadcasts from Europe, Asia, and Australia. Yet so far we've heard very few. Why?"

The same question had bothered Donovan. He shrugged. "Who knows? Maybe we're being too optimistic. Maybe there are pathetically few survivors."

"Maybe the war deranged the atmospheric conditions to such an extent that there is too much interference," Alex added. "There could be people out there trying to get through who simply can't."

"We'll know more soon," Donovan stated. "We'll travel all the way up the Eastern Seaboard and see what's cooking."

Alex grimaced. "Poor choice of words."

"Sorry."

Executive Officer Percy cleared his throat. "Initially, I thought I'd be excited about going back, but I'm not. I might have been better off staying on Espiritu and helping to hunt down those animals."

The surprising disclosure prompted Donovan to stare at his second-in-command. "What makes you say a thing like that?"

"Because many of us have fam—" Percy began, then stopped and corrected himself. "*Had* families or other relatives and loved ones living on the East Coast. Most of us have resigned ourselves to the fact they're all dead. Going back will only rub our noses in it, so to speak. We'll have to relive our hurt all over again."

"It can't be helped," Donovan stated, thinking of his own parents and their home in New York City. Both they and the house were now undoubtedly radioactive ashes. "We can't run from reality. Like it or not, we must seek out survivors wherever they may be. We have a responsibility to them, and to all our loved ones who died so needlessly, to salvage what we can from the rubble and rebuild."

"I know," Percy said, "but the knowledge doesn't make the doing any easier."

The somber conversation silenced them for a while, stimulating troubled thoughts long suppressed. They surveyed the sea, watching dolphins frolic and shark fins cruise past. A small flock of gulls was sighted flying from east to west.

"If it wasn't for all the damn sharks, you'd never know there had been a war," Alex remarked bitterly to break the ice.

"In San Francisco the problem was wolves," Percy said. "I wonder what type of predators we'll find in New York."

"White-shirts," Donovan stated.

"Maybe not," Alex said. "Remember, Peter believes that, from a strictly biological perspective, the white-shirts are literal zombies. The walking dead. Their brains have stopped functioning but their bodies plod on, and he doesn't think their bodies can sustain them indefinitely. Eventually the toxins in their systems and the psychosis disease will wipe out all of them."

"Eventually," Donovan said bitterly. "Is that before or after they've killed every last survivor?"

She had no answer for that one.

13

"Thank you for coming over to fix the door."

Charlie gave Betty Thompson his most devil-may-care smile and shrugged. "What are friends for? Besides, all I had to do was level off the bottom so it wouldn't jam." He hefted the plane in his right hand and opened and closed the front door again to impress her with his competence. "See? Doesn't stick a bit."

"I never was much good with tools," Betty said, her eyes lingering affectionately on his.

Tingling all over, Charlie knelt and replaced the plane in the gray toolbox he had borrowed from one of the colonists. "Where are the kids?" he inquired casually. "Haven't seen them around all afternoon."

"Melanie is at a girlfriend's and Stevie went over to play with one of his buddies," Betty said, and gazed out the window of her living room at a group of colonists a few dozen yards away who were engaged in idle conversation. One of them laughed. "It's hard to believe everything has returned to normal so quickly."

Rising, Charlie followed the direction of her gaze. "It's only because there hasn't been a sign of the man-eaters since the original attacks. We keep hearing the howling and things moving about in the jungle at night, but the animals won't show themselves. Two nights ago we set out bait, but still no luck."

"Bait?"

"Gutted fish and a dead monkey Richards shot. We were hoping the scent of blood would draw the things in."

Betty looked out the window again. "It'll be dark in an hour or so. What will you try next?"

"I don't have the foggiest. We toyed with the notion of building a trap, a cage with a door that can be sprung when an animal takes the food inside. But if the creatures won't take the bait now, they sure as hell won't touch anything we put in a cage."

An absent nod was Betty's response. She stared at his hair, his mouth, and his neck, then bowed her head. "You know, if we keep seeing each other every day people are bound to talk."

"Let them. Who cares?"

Betty moved a little closer. "I don't," she said, and raised her head.

"Neither do I," Charlie said softly, and took her into his arms. She offered no resistance when he kissed her. Instead, her lips parted and her tongue flicked out to touch his. He savored the sweet taste of her and felt himself stir, his skin feeling warm, his heart thumping to beat the band. At last he drew back and smiled. "This is starting to get serious."

"I don't mind if you don't."

"Not at all."

"Just go slow. Be patient. I'm still not over—" Betty began, her inner hurt mirrored in her face.

Charlie interrupted to spare her the pain of explaining about her affection for her late husband. "I understand. Don't worry. I'm not about to put pressure on you. Our motto will be Easy Does It."

"Thanks," Betty said, smiling.

For a moment they let their eyes convey their feelings, and then Charlie coughed lightly and stepped back. "I'd best be on my way. I have to get ready for tonight." He leaned down and lifted the toolbox.

"You be careful."

"I will," Charlie said, walking to the front door. She

followed him outside. "Say hi to the kids for me."

"Will do." Betty idly stared eastward and pointed. "Look. There goes your new buddy."

Charlie pivoted and saw Baltimore Jack thirty yards away, strolling to the south. "What makes you say that?" he asked defensively.

"Every time I turn around I see the two of you together. I think everyone has noticed."

"Yeah. Well, it's not my doing. He dogs my tracks like an overgrown puppy."

"You don't sound very pleased about it."

"I'm not. A person likes to choose their own friends, not have someone latch onto them like a leech."

Betty looked at the wrestler. "If he's bothering you, why not tell him to his face?"

"Because I don't want to hurt the man's feelings," Charlie admitted. "Basically he's a decent guy. I just feel uncomfortable having him hang around. Did you know he keeps me company when I'm on patrol?"

"No, I didn't."

"Yep. Started a few nights ago. I've tried to be tactful and tell him he doesn't have to walk with me, but he insists on tagging along." Charlie frowned. "What am I supposed to do? Order him to stay indoors? I doubt I have the right. So it looks as if I'm stuck with him for the time being."

"Give it time. Maybe he's going through a phase of some kind and it will wear off."

Charlie chuckled. "I think he's catching up on all the time he spent alone on this island. Deep down he likes associating with other people."

"Maybe some good will come of it," Betty suggested.

"I can't imagine what," Charlie said dryly, and gave a wave as he started to walk away. "I'll see you tomorrow."

"Can you make it for lunch?"

"You bet, even if I have to give up some of my beauty sleep."

Betty blew him a kiss and went inside.

Feeling as if his heart were floating on air, Charlie walked toward the hut belonging to the colonist who'd loaned him the tools. He whistled happily, glad to be alive. Who would have thought it? Who would have figured he'd fall head over heels for a widow with two children? What was it about her that made Betty so special? Her figure? No, he'd known women with shapelier bods. Her personality? Yep. That had to be a big part of the attraction. He enjoyed every minute spent with her, which was more than he could say about spending time with, say, Baltimore Jack.

The thought of the wrestler brought a lopsided grin to his face. His gunnery detail had taken to teasing him about Jack. Richards had gone so far as to label the giant as Charlie's official bodyguard or baby-sitter. "Take your pick."

In a way Charlie felt sorry for the big guy. From their conversations it was obvious that killing the Russian wrestler had affected Jack in many ways. Where once the giant was outgoing, he withdrew into a shell. Where once Jack was afraid of nothing, he became afraid of himself, of his own strength. Where once the giant had viewed the world in rosy terms of good and bad and seen the globe as his personal playground, the death shattered that perception and replaced it with a cold cynicism and a belief that the forces controlling the cosmos were neutral observers instead of diligently working for the betterment of all. The war had only served to reinforce Jack's doubts.

He glanced westward at the sun and hurried his steps, eager to enjoy a hearty snack before going on duty. They would set out bait again tonight. Not that it would do any good. It was as if the things *knew* someone was gunning for them and were deliberately staying away. The idea, of course, was ludicrous, but he had entertained the notion on more than one occasion. Why else were the animals being so elusive again?

Charlie returned the toolbox and headed for his own place. He thought of Tom and wondered how his brother was faring. A certain part of him longed to be on *Liberator*, cruising into the heart of adventure and confronting the unknown. But then Betty's laughing features materialized in his mind's eye and he was glad he'd stayed behind. Some things were more important than an adrenaline rush.

In two minutes he reached his hut. After eating, he slung his Franchi over one arm, double-checked the clip in his pistol, fastened the transceiver to his belt, and stepped outdoors just as the sun touched the western horizon. He strolled northward. The prearranged meeting place for the detail was at the midpoint of the north fence.

Richards, Wayne, and Kent were already there, chuckling as Richards regaled them with tales of women he had known in various ports of call. All three glanced around at the sound of Charlie's approach.

"Forsooth, is that noble Romeo who approacheth?" Richards called out.

The others cackled.

"Forsooth your ass," Charlie said.

Richards winked at his companions and asked in feigned innocence, "Have you ever noticed how certain guys lose their sense of humor when they fall for a shapely wench?"

"I'll be sure and tell Betty that you called her a wench," Charlie stated. "And I want to be there when she belts you."

"See what I mean?" Richards said to Wayne and Kent.

Charlie stepped to the fence and scanned the jungle.

"All right. Enough goofing off. Did anyone bring bait for tonight?"

"Yes, sir," Wayne replied. "Parker caught six fish today. We can use those."

"Good. When Parker gets here we'll let Mr. Richards hang them from a tree."

"Uh, sir?" Wayne said.

Charlie looked at him. "What?"

Seaman Wayne pointed to the northeast.

Pivoting, Charlie was surprised to spy Parker twenty-five feet away in the act of tying the string of fish to a low limb. Damn. Why hadn't he seen him before?

"Anything else you'd like us to do, sir?" Richards asked with a straight face.

"Do you know that cliff north of the volcano?" Charlie inquired somberly, giving them a taste of their own medicine.

"Yes, sir?"

"Go jump off it."

This time Wayne and Kent chuckled at Richards's expense.

Charlie faced them, about to tell them to assume their posts, when he saw two women hurrying in their direction. One of the women was Betty Thompson, her expression reflecting intense anxiety. He took several steps and hailed them. "What's up?"

"Stevie and Timmy are missing," Betty answered.

Missing? Charlie hastened to meet them, his men following. He tried to remember the name of the other woman. Edith Flores, wasn't it? They'd only met once and he couldn't be sure.

"We've searched everywhere," Betty said when still ten feet off. "Stevie went over to Timmy's to play. They asked Edith if they could go outside and she told them they could provided they stayed near her hut. Now they're gone."

Charlie stopped and looked at Edith. "How old is your son?"

"Six, the same as Stevie."

"Could they be with your husband?"

"No. Tony was with me. He's scouring the village now."

"He'll probably find them playing somewhere," Charlie assured them. "You know how boys that age can be. They wander off all the time."

Betty wrung her hands and frowned. "It might be worse than that. Earlier today Stevie was nagging me to go to the beach. I haven't let him since the attacks. He had a fit when I said no, and I suggested he go play with Timmy to take his mind off it."

"Timmy has been bugging me about the beach, too," Edith Flores chimed in. "In fact, they both begged me to take them after Stevie came over today."

"And you figure they took off when you let them go out to play," Charlie deduced. "Okay. We'll check it out."

"Please," Edith said.

"But which beach do you think they headed for?" Charlie asked. The one to the south was closer but the strip of sand on the northeast tip of the island was also a favorite.

"I doubt they'd take it into their little heads to go to the northeast beach," Betty said. "It's too far away."

"I agree," Edith stated.

"Okay." Charlie looked over his shoulder to find that Seaman Parker had joined them. "You heard the ladies. Let's go." He smiled encouragement at Betty and jogged southward, glancing to the west where the sun had dipped halfway below the horizon. Twilight would descend soon, and with the coming of night the man-eaters would be abroad.

A bronzed figure in white shorts ran from between two huts and came over to Charlie, keeping pace with fluid ease, a friendly smile curling his lips. "Howdy, little buddy. Where are you going in such a hurry?"

Charlie glanced at the wrestler and tried to keep from letting his annoyance show. He didn't want Jack tagging along; the man would probably only get in the way. But since there was no time to stop and argue about it, he resigned himself to the inevitable and said, "Two boys are missing. We're on our way to find them."

"Can I come along?"

Charlie hesitated, wishing he had the courage to tell the guy no.

"Please," Baltimore Jack requested softly.

Again Charlie looked up at him, and he was surprised to detect obvious pleading in the wrestler's eyes. "Sure," he said. "You're welcome to help."

"Thanks."

They drew curious stares from the many colonists they passed, several of whom hailed them, wanting to know what was going on. Charlie waved and told them he would explain later.

A band of jungle separated the village from the south side of Espiritu, and a well-worn path led from the huts to the sea. Birds and parrots were voicing their farewell chorus to the fading day, while monkeys frolicked in the trees, swinging from limb to limb and chattering noisily.

Charlie hoped the boys were playing somewhere in the village. Not that he thought they were in any danger until the sun went down, but his vaunted intuition was flaring again, filling him with a feeling of dread. Must be a bad case of nerves, he figured, and let it go at that.

Before long the south expanse of beach appeared before their expectant eyes and they burst from the path to halt in consternation. There wasn't a soul in sight. Gulls, petrels, and other seabirds soared sluggishly on the air currents or walked at the water's edge seeking crabs and fish.

"Fan out," Charlie ordered. He cupped his hands to his mouth and shouted, "Stevie! Timmy! Where are you?"

Only a gull screeched stridently in response.

The men moved in different directions, scouring the shoreline, all except for Baltimore Jack. He stayed at Charlie's side and voiced a question.

"Stevie? Would that be Stevie Thompson?"

"Yeah."

"And what is Timmy's last name?"

"Flores."

"Oh. I know his parents. Antonio and Edith, right?"

"Yeah," Charlie said, bothered by the queries, trying to concentrate on surveying the border of the jungle to their east. Maybe the boys were playing in the trees.

"Mr. Donovan," Seaman Kent called out formally. "Tracks, sir."

Charlie hastened to where Kent stood within a yard of the ocean. There, recently imprinted in the damp sand, were the tracks of two small, naked feet heading westward.

"It has to be them," Baltimore Jack stated.

"Darn kids," Charlie muttered, and motioned to the others. "Let's go!" He moved out, running alongside the footprints, and gazed at the far horizon, at the sun that was steadily sinking. The upper rim had yet to disappear. Don't worry, he told himself. There's still plenty of time.

The trail led along the water's edge for several hundred yards, then angled across the beach to the jungle. The prints were easy to follow, even in the dry sand farther from the ocean, until the search party reached the treeline.

Charlie halted in midstride and vented an oath. "Son of a bitch!" The tracks vanished in the weeds and the boys were nowhere in sight.

Seaman Richards peered into the dense vegetation.

"Don't they know better than to go waltzing around in the jungle alone?"

"We'll spread out in pairs. Call their names as often as you can," Charlie directed. "Richards and Wayne, go northeast. Kent, you and Parker head due north." He looked at Jack. "How about if you and I got northwest?"

"Fine by me."

Quickly they hastened away, each man acutely conscious of the gradually deepening darkness.

Unslinging his Franchi, Charlie maintained a reckless pace. Both he and Jack repeatedly yelled the boys' names, with no results. Through the trees to the northwest loomed the smoking cone, an ominous backdrop to their search.

Five minutes elapsed. Ten. The shouts of the other pairs became fainter and fainter. Cowed by the vocal invasion, the wildlife was keeping quiet. A blanket of near-total silence lay heavy on the landscape.

Then Charlie heard new sounds that made his blood run cold: the panicked cries of terrified boys mingled with the savage growls of fierce beasts.

Alex found him on the topside bridge, his silhouette unmistakable against the backdrop of glittering stars. He was leaning on the rail and gazing westward with that forlorn puppyish look she found so attractive. Engrossed in his reflections, he didn't even realize she had climbed from the hatch until she walked up behind him and covered his eyes with her hands. "Guess who, sailor? And if you guess correctly this could be your lucky night."

Donovan coughed lightly, turned, and nodded toward the rear of the bridge.

Puzzled by his lack of enthusiasm, Alex glanced around and spied the crewman assigned to the night watch, an ensign who had developed an inordinate interest in the stern. "Whoops," she said softly.

"What are you doing up here?" Donovan asked. "I thought you were sound asleep."

"I was, until I rolled over to put my arm around you and all I hugged was your pillow," Alex replied. "Was my snoring too loud?"

"No louder than a diesel motor."

"Do you know it's after one A.M.?"

"But only after nine Espiritu time."

"Don't evade the issue," Alex chided him.

"Which is?"

"What the hell are you doing out here at this time of night?"

Shifting so he could gaze westward again in the direction of Central America, Donovan sighed. "Not a peep. Not one damn peep. We should have heard something. There used to be a powerful shortwave station in Honduras at Tegucigalpa. Nicaragua had a five-kilowatt station. And we should be picking up Mexico by now. Hell, in Mexico City there were half a dozen shortwave stations with ten kilowatts or more." He paused and repeated, "Not a peep. And of course nothing on the AM or FM bands, either."

"This is what has you down in the dumps?"

"I guess so," Donovan said. "It's hard to put my finger on it. Maybe I'm just fully waking up to how dead the world really is."

"It's a terrible feeling to think you're all alone in the world," Alex concurred. Despite the presence of the watch officer, she tenderly stroked his cheek.

"We've been so busy since the war with one thing or another, there hasn't been a chance for the consequences to completely sink in. They have now. When I stand next to Jennings and listen to all that static on the airwaves it's enough to give me goose bumps."

"Any word yet from Ronca and Hardesty?"

"No."

"There's always tomorrow. If they're running low on battery power, then the closer we get to New York the more likely we are to pick them up."

"If they're still there," Donovan said morosely.

Alex had never heard such forlorn melancholy in his tone before, and suddenly she perceived the real reason for his recent, uncharacteristic depression. "You think they're dead, don't you?"

"It's a possibility."

"True. And you're blaming yourself."

"If I hadn't dragged my heels back on Espiritu, we could have rescued them a couple of weeks ago."

"You did what you thought was best."

Donovan nodded, his eyes on the sea. "Small consolation if those families have perished."

"If you ask me, you're letting your commitment to rescue all survivors get the better of you."

"How do you mean?"

"You're not going to be able to save every one. The sooner you own up to your limitations, the better off you'll be. You're trying to bear the weight of the world on your shoulders, Tom, and you're only human."

They stood side by side for a while, staring off into the distance. The moon cast a pale glow over the placid water, and a mild northwesterly breeze caressed their faces. Occasionally splashing noises were heard as fish leaped clear of the water and dived again.

"Sorry," Donovan said at last. "I guess I have been letting it get to me."

"Lighten up. You've got to learn to relax, to be more like your brother. Charlie never has a care in the world."

The boys were screeching in unison at the tops of their lungs and the snarls of the man-eaters had attained a crescendo of primal ferocity when Charlie and Baltimore Jack burst from the undergrowth into a spacious clearing and halted.

Charlie took one look and blurted out, "Son of a bitch!"

In the center of the clearing reared a towering tree, and clinging desperately to one of its lower branches were Stevie and Timmy, their legs dangling just above the furious leaps of the nine beasts milling wildly about underneath them.

"They're dogs," Baltimore Jack declared. "Nothing but a pack of lousy dogs."

"Yeah," Charlie said in astonishment. But they were dogs unlike any ever bred in civilization.

The feral canines were the size of German shepherds. Their thin coats were of various hues, with browns, blacks, and mottled coats predominating. They possessed stocky bodies, supported by squat, powerful legs, and long, busy tails. Like shepherds, they had broad, angular heads. Pointed rows of saliva-covered teeth were exposed when they growled or snarled or snapped at the boys.

Charlie went to employ the Franchi and thought better of the idea. With Stevie and Timmy so close to the pack, a stray round might well hit them. Instead he drew his pistol.

"I'll get the boys," Baltimore Jack rashly declared, and dashed forward.

"No!" Charlie cried, too late.

The shout drew the attention of the dogs, who abruptly froze in their tracks and glanced around, balefully regarding the intruders. In the subdued light they resembled prehistoric wolves, majestic and terrible.

"Help us!" Stevie wailed.

"Don't worry," Jack yelled. "We're here." He waved his arms overhead and bellowed at the pack. "Get lost! Go on! Get out of here!"

The dogs charged.

Charlie saw the biggest beast of all surge toward the wrestler, the rest on its heels, and he darted to the right, increasing the angle and giving himself a better shot. He extended his right arm and sighted on the big brute, the apparent leader, taking a bead on its chest, not an easy task to do when the dog was practically flying over the ground. Only eight feet separated the dog from the wrestler when he squeezed the trigger.

A booming retort filled the clearing, and at the sound the leader toppled in a headlong roll of limbs and tail to finally stop at the very feet of the giant, dead.

A second dog closed in, and a second shot downed it.

Then a third dog launched itself into the air, going for the wrestler's throat.

Charlie tried to snap off a shot, but there was no time. He saw Baltimore Jack draw back a brawny fist and deliver a devastating right to the tip of the dog's nose. The blow propelled the beast to the ground, where it lay still, dazed.

Unexpectedly, the remaining pack members whirled and ran into the jungle, scattering in all directions.

Tracking one, Charlie was about to squeeze the trigger when the beast loped into the dense brush. Rather than snap off a hasty shot he held his fire. The last thing he wanted was an injured feral dog roaming the island; injured predators were known to be far more dangerous than they would be normally. He ran to the tree and got there a few strides behind the giant.

"You're safe now," Baltimore Jack told the shaking boys. He plucked them from the limb as if they were peaches instead of weighing close to fifty pounds each.

Timmy was bawling his brains out.

Stevie sniffled, glanced at Charlie, and yelled, "Let me go! Let me go!"

Startled, Baltimore Jack complied.

The instant Stevie's feet touched the ground he stepped over and threw his arms around Charlie's legs. "Thank you! Thank you! Thank you!" he declared. "You saved us, Mr. Donovan."

Taken aback by the show of affection, Charlie slung the Franchi over his left arm and placed his left hand on the boy's shoulders. "Jack helped," he mentioned. "And call me Charlie, will you?"

Stevie looked up, his cheeks streaked with tears, and grinned. "Sure, Charlie. I can't wait for you to be my new dad."

The shocking disclosure was no sooner uttered than Baltimore Jack pointed and bellowed, "Look!"

Charlie swung around, nearly tripping over his own feet because of Stevie's grip on his legs, and spotted the dog that had been dazed by the giant scrambling erect. Automatically he aimed the pistol and squeezed off a shot.

Struck in the head, the dog unexpectedly leaped straight up into the air and crashed down again. Its legs twitched and its mouth opened and closed spasmodically. After a bit the animal ceased moving altogether.

"Maybe we should get out of here in case the pack decides to come back," Baltimore Jack proposed.

"Good idea," Charlie agreed, and scooped Stevie into his left arm. "Hang on tight."

"You bet."

Charlie led the way, heading in the general direction of the village, weaving among trees and avoiding vines.

"Were you looking for us?" Stevie asked.

"Yep," Charlie answered, his eyes darting right and left, wary of being attacked again.

"Did my mom send you?"

"Yep."

"Uh-oh. I'm in trouble, aren't I?"

"*Big* trouble."

"Darn. All we wanted to do was take a hike."

"You nearly got yourselves killed."

"I know," Stevie said sadly. "We heard the dogs coming and climbed into that tree, but we couldn't get high enough in time."

From up ahead came the shouts of the four crewmen.

"Charlie! Where are you?"

"Can you hear us?"

"Baltimore Jack? What's all the shooting?"

"We're all right!" Charlie responded as he ran. He glanced at the boy, thinking he might never have a better opportunity. "Say, Stevie?"

"Yeah?"

"What did you mean about my becoming your dad?"

"My sister says you may be our new daddy. That is, if Mom is warm for your form."

Charlie almost tripped again. "Were those her words?"

"Yeah. Aren't girls weird?"

"Yep. Especially big sisters."

Seaman Richards's voice came from near at hand. "Charlie? Jack? Where the hell are you?"

"Here," Charlie replied. Moments later he spied the four men sprinting toward him. He slowed and so did they.

"What was all the shooting, sir?" Kent asked when they met and halted.

"We discovered the identity of the man-eaters," Charlie revealed. "A pack of wild dogs."

"Dogs?" Wayne repeated in disbelief. "Did you say dogs?"

"We'll sort it all out later," Charlie said. "Right now we must get these boys to their parents. They've been scared to death. The four of you bring up the rear and stay frosty."

Immediately the quartet moved to comply.

Charlie looked at the wrestler, who had an oddly peaceful expression on his face, and started off again. Now that he knew dogs were the culprits, he could take appropriate measures to wipe them out. The pack must have a lair somewhere on Espiritu. All he had to do was find it.

First, though, maybe he should have a *long* talk with Betty Thompson.

15

Twenty-two hours after leaving the Panama Canal *Liberator* neared the south tip of Florida. An almost palpable tension gripped the crew as the ship drew closer to the Eastern Seaboard. Not one man was willing to accept that America had been completely destroyed. The idea that every city had been obliterated and every man, woman, and child vaporized was ludicrous, as the highly educated seamen knew. Even if all the primary targets in the country had been hit with surface bursts, there were many areas where no fallout whatever would fall and large regions where the probability of receiving marginal fallout was less than 2 percent. There *must* be survivors.

Donovan sat in his swivel chair studying the screen. Beside him stood Alex. "Reduce speed to fifty knots, Mr. Hooper."

"Aye, Captain."

"Maintain a course of zero-nine-zero degrees until we're due south of Key West."

"Will do, sir."

Resting his right elbow on the chair, Donovan noted their position with satisfaction. *Liberator* was passing through the Straits of Florida, cruising in the main channel at a depth of 300 feet. The bottom of the sea lay another 5,730 feet below. There were no submerged seamounts or guyots to worry about. Soon they would pass the Florida Keys, a group of islands that curved in a line from southern Florida southwest into the Gulf. Beyond lay the eastern half of the Straits, including the shallower waters of the Great Bahama Bank.

"I still can't believe the readings on Cuba," Alex commented thoughtfully.

"Havana will be hot for a thousand years," Donovan agreed, thinking of the long-range scanning conducted hours ago when the sub was at the north end of the Yucatan Channel. The radiation readings had gone off the scale.

"Do you think many cities in the United States are as bad?"

"Those near major military installations, most definitely. The rest, it's hard to say. It all depends on whether air bursts or surface bursts were used."

"Refresh my memory. Is there a big difference?"

Donovan grinned. "I thought you're supposed to be our whiz of a science officer."

"Science, yes. Nuclear warfare and general stupidity, no."

"Okay. A surface burst produces far more fallout but an air burst is a more effective way to damage a big city."

"Because the surface burst spews tons of dirt and debris up into the radioactive cloud and all these particles descend to the ground as fallout, whereas an air burst takes place high in the atmosphere, sucks up no dirt or debris, and produces virtually no fallout, although the concussive force of the blast pulverizes whatever is below," Alex stated, sounding as if she was quoting from a reference book.

"I thought you said you didn't know anything about nuclear war."

"I remembered browsing through a book my father owned a few years ago. Something about surviving Doomsday. When I read that paragraph, I laughed and put the book down. I couldn't see where there was any big difference between dying of lingering radiation poisoning or being reduced to ashes in the blink of an eye."

"The first way is a lot slower and a lot more painful."

"Dead is dead. How a person dies is incidental."

"I don't agree," Donovan said. "I'd rather go quick than slow."

Suddenly Jennings interrupted. "Captain, we're picking up a broadcast."

Donovan flew to the communications station. "Put it on the speaker."

Jenning flicked a toggle and pressed a button. Immediately static crackled from a speaker on the console to his right. Faint in the background was the sound of a male voice, the words indistinguishable.

"Can you amplify the voice?"

"I'll try to filter out the interference," Jennings said, and worked a dial. Seconds later the static disappeared.

" . . . on our last legs. If anyone can hear me, please respond," the man stated with a decided Southern accent. "This is Brick Wilson in Argyle," he went on wearily, as if he had been broadcasting the same message for hours. "There are thirty-one folks here with me and we're under attack from the crazies. We're trapped and can't get out unless we get help. Is anyone listening?"

"He's broadcasting on the shortwave band at five thousand kilocycles," Jennings disclosed. "The signal is real weak. For better reception we need to raise the receiving mast."

"Consider it done," Donovan said, pivoting. "Mr. Hooper, slow to ten knots and bring us to the surface."

"Yes sir."

"Where in the world is Argyle?" Alex wondered.

"Mr. Jennings, ask the computer," Donovan directed.

The communications officer typed in the appropriate request on the keyboard and in moments the monitor displayed a map of Georgia. A bright red dot indicated the location of Argyle, a tiny town only thirty miles north of the Florida border. Between the town and the Sunshine State lay the vast Okefenokee Swamp.

"It's way out in the boonies," Jennings said.

"Which explains why there are survivors," Alex commented.

"But maybe not for long," Donovan said grimly.

They listened expectantly for the broadcast to be repeated but the speaker mocked them with its silence. Everyone on the bridge had their gaze fixed on the communications station.

"Let's try to raise them," Donovan said. "Give me a microphone."

Jennings handed one over and worked his console. "All set, but I doubt they will hear us until we're on the surface."

"No harm in trying," Donovan said, and pressed the mike switch. "This is Captain Thomas P. Donovan of the U.S.S. *Liberator* calling Argyle, Georgia. Do you read me?"

There was no response.

Shortly thereafter Helmsman Hooper announced the words they were most eager to hear.

"We're on the surface, Captain."

"Good. Mr. Percy, get a watch officer topside."

"Perhaps two would be better, sir," the executive officer responded. "We want to be extra sharp from here on out."

"Makes sense. Do it," Donovan said, and turned to Jennings. "Up with the receiving mast."

A button was promptly stabbed. "Mast up. Boosting the gain to the max."

The speaker only hissed softly.

"I'll try again," Donovan proposed, and did so. "This is Captain Tom Donovan calling Argyle, Georgia. Do you copy? Over."

"Yes! Yes! Oh, God! Yes!" came the answer from over 550 miles away. "This is Brick Wilson in Argyle. We read you! We read you!"

Shouts of spontaneous delight erupted on the bridge, and Donovan had to motion for silence. When the shouts ceased Wilson could be heard speaking a mile a minute.

". . . are you? Did you say you're a captain? We need help and we need it bad. How soon can you get here? Are you still there?"

"I'm still here," Donovan assured him. "Calm down and I'll take your questions one at a time. Yes, I'm a captain, and I'm in command of a nuclear-powered sub currently in the Straits of Florida. Over."

"A submarine? And you're one of ours? I mean, you're really American?" Wilson asked, his tone laced with quivering relief. "Sweet Jesus, our prayers have been answered."

"What is your situation there? We understand there are others with you and you're under attack?"

"Yes. There are hundreds of zombies outside the walls. Sooner or later they'll breach our defenses."

"What do you mean by zombies?"

"That's just our name for them. We figure the radiation or one of those chemical weapons turned lots of people into mindless killing machines. They all wear white and they roam the countryside murdering everyone who is still normal. Hell, we've even seen them slaughter dogs and cats."

Executive Officer Percy made a hissing noise. "The damn white-shirts again."

Donovan cleared his throat. "How long do you think you can hold out, Mr. Wilson?"

"Call me Brick. Not much longer, Captain. We're holed up at Milo Ferguson's place. Milo's house is set on two acres and there are stone walls ten feet high surrounding the property. So far we've been able to keep the zombies out, although they've tried twenty or thirty times to get through the iron gate. They're not too bright. They've been—"

Faint static suddenly crackled from the speaker.

"Brick, are you still there?" Donovan asked urgently.

"Yep. Sorry, Captain. Billy Bob just told me those things are trying to get in again. Where was I? Oh, yeah. They've been out there for a month now, and it didn't occur to them to stack things up at the base of the wall and try to climb over until a couple of days ago. Even so, they're so slow about it we have time to knock the stuff down using long poles." Brick paused. "But there are more and more of them every day. It's only a matter of time until they get in."

Frowning, Donovan studied the map of Georgia. Argyle was a good sixty miles inland from the Atlantic Ocean. With the white-shirts everywhere, the prospect of a rescue detail getting through was remote.

"How soon can you get here, Captain?" Brick inquired anxiously.

Donovan looked at Alex, then at the computer monitor. "I don't think you should count on us."

"What?"

"We can be off the Georgia coast in about eight or nine hours, but you're too far inland for me to risk sending in any of my men."

"You can't be serious. We have women and children here. What kind of monster are you?"

"Try to understand. I have a small crew. I couldn't afford to send more than five or six men after you at the most. What chance would they have to get through?"

Brick fell silent. A full minute elapsed before he spoke again, his voice strained, sounding like a man devoid of all hope. "I see what you mean. They wouldn't have a snowball's chance in hell. Damn. We're history."

"Don't give up yet," Donovan urged. "There might be something we can do to help. I'll call you back in an hour and let you know what we come up with."

"Thanks. Appreciate it. Brick Wilson over and out."

Acutely miserable at having let the man down, Donovan lowered the mike to the console. He started to turn and nearly bumped into Percy.

"Captain, request permission to lead a squad to Argyle."

"No."

"Begging your pardon, sir, but we have to try and save those poor people."

"I can't afford to lose more men, Mr. Percy. You know how critical our manpower situation is. We're already five men short because we left my brother and his gunnery detail on Espiritu. If you go off with another six men, that's about one fourth of our crew missing. What if we run into an emergency situation ourselves?"

"We can't just abandon them to the white-shirts," Percy obstinately persisted.

Alex touched Donovan's arm. "Why don't we have a staff meeting and discuss our options? Like you said, there might be something we can do."

"Agreed. Mr. Jennings, contact Flazy and Dr. Fisher. I want them to meet us in the galley in five minutes."

"Aye, Skipper."

Donovan hastened from the bridge with Alex and Percy in tow. He was conscious of the critical stares directed his way by many of his men, and he couldn't blame them one bit. Rescuing survivors was their primary objective. He'd preached as much time and again. And now here he was apparently turning his back on a group desperately in need of help. But what else could he do?

Chief Engineer Smith was approaching from the opposite direction.

"Flazy, you must be a mind reader."

Smith halted and blinked. "What?"

"I just told Jennings to find you. We're holding a staff meeting in the galley right away and I need your input."

"Sounds urgent. What's up?"

"It's time for me to put my money where my mouth is."

"Huh?"

Charlie had only been in bed an hour when the light knock sounded on his front door. He opened his eyes, still drowsy and sluggish, and listened, uncertain whether he'd really heard the noise or if he'd imagined it. When the second knock came he sat up, yawned, and ran his right hand through his tousled hair. Since he didn't want to greet his visitor in his underwear, he slowly wiggled his legs into his pants and shuffled from the messy bedroom.

Again the person knocked.

"Coming," Charlie called out. "Hold your horses." He reached the door and yanked it wide, expecting to find one of his men or his ever-faithful companion Baltimore Jack.

"Hi," Betty Thompson said nervously.

Charlie was instantly awake. "Hello," he said.

"Did I wake you? I was hoping I'd get here before you fell asleep. I know you like to sleep until one or two in the afternoon after a night of guard duty."

"No," Charlie lied. "I wasn't asleep yet."

"May I come in?"

"Sure," Charlie said, and quickly stepped aside to let her enter. He stood with his hand on the knob and noticed she had her hands clasped tightly together. "What's up? Is Stevie off on another nature stroll?"

Betty laughed. "No. He's fine. Melanie and him are staying with Edith today. I want to thank you again for saving his life."

"There's no need. You've thanked me two dozen times already."

"Have the hunting parties had any luck locating the dogs' lair?"

"Not yet. This is a big island. But we'll wipe them out eventually."

"The kids in the village sure have taken a liking to Jack. He's a big hero now with them, almost as big a hero as you are."

"Yeah." Charlie smiled. "Timmy idolizes the guy. It's worked wonders on Jack's disposition."

Nodding, Betty gazed around the room. "Nice place you've got here."

Charlie abruptly perceived she was making small talk to mask an underlying current of anxiety reflected in her expression and her posture. "Are you all right? Is anything wrong?"

"Never felt better." Betty looked him in the eyes. "Are you planning to stand there all day like a dummy or are you going back to bed?"

Astonishment hit him like a ton of bricks when the full significance of her question hit home. He gaped, then blurted, "Are you sure?"

"You could take some lessons from Rhett Butler," Betty quipped, beaming. "Of course I'm sure. I wouldn't be here if I wasn't. So what are you going to do?"

Charlie closed the door so fast he accidentally slammed it.

Vibrant tension charged the climate-controlled atmosphere on the bridge as *Liberator* prowled up Saint Andrew Sound toward Brunswick, Georgia.

Donovan sat rigidly in his duty chair, eyes riveted to the screen. "Do we have plenty of clearance under the keel, Mr. Jennings?"

"Yes, sir. Currently seventy-five feet and holding."

"Good. Mr. Hooper, steady as she goes at fifteen knots."

"Aye, Captain."

"We're not getting a thing out of Brunswick, sir," Jennings reported. "No radio, no shortwave, no television, microwave, nothing."

"Thank you. Any hot spots?"

"No, sir. Radiation levels are slightly elevated, but not enough to pose a health threat even with prolonged exposure. Any fallout that fell must have been dispersed by the wind or soaked into the soil by the heavy rains common in this region."

"Distance to Brunswick?" Donovan asked.

"Five miles."

"Close enough," Donovan said. "Mr. Hooper, take us as close as you can to the south shore."

"Taking us in, Captain."

Executive Officer Percy stepped onto the bridge dressed in a skintight black bodysuit. Crisscrossing his chest were two utility belts containing spare magazines for the Franchi he held in his left hand and extra clips for the two Colts strapped around his waist, while in various other belt pockets were his rations, rope, a compass, matches, and the other gear he would require. Attached to clips on the outer edges of the belts were a half dozen grenades. Affixed to his belt behind his left holster was a transceiver.

Behind Percy came Seaman Burroughs, a stocky crewman with blond hair and blue eyes, similarly attired except for a large brown leather bag slung over his right shoulder.

Donovan watched them approach and mustered a smile of encouragement. "You look as if you're ready to kick butt."

"I feel ready," Percy replied. "And I want to thank you for letting us go in."

"The decision was unanimous. And wait to thank me until you're safe and sound back on the ship," Donovan said. He glanced at the seaman. "Do you have everything you'll need?"

"I'm ready and raring to go, sir," Burroughs assured him, and patted the bag. "We have enough extra goodies to wipe out an army."

Donovan turned to Percy. "Okay. Let's go over the plan again."

"Once more? We've already been through it a dozen times, Skipper."

"Humor me."

"All right. We're to find a car or truck that still runs, which shouldn't be too hard if there are as many abandoned vehicles here as there were in San Francisco and elsewhere. Then we head like bats out of hell to Argyle—"

"The route?" Donovan interrupted.

"There's not much to it. We take U.S. Highway Eighty-four to Waycross, use the bypass to skirt the town, then continue on Eighty-four until we hit Argyle.

About seventy-fives miles, all told. Barring unforeseen difficulties we should be there about ninety minutes after we find our transportation."

Donovan nodded. "Once you're there, do as you see fit. If you can't help those people don't sacrifice yourselves. But if you bail them out, you'll have thirty-five hours to reach the rendezvous point. It'll take us at least that long to get to New York and return." He stared at the screen, noting the proximity of the south bank.

"We can handle it, Captain."

"I just wish we could spare more men." Donovan consulted his watch. "It's almost twenty-two hundred hours. Ten P.M. The white-shirts, if there are any in this area, will have their bonfires going by now. They'll be easy to spot and avoid."

"Don't worry, Skipper. We're not going to let the crazies get their putrid hands on us."

Donovan tried not to let his anxiety show. "I sincerely hope they don't, John," he said, and added for emphasis, "I sincerely hope they don't."

Percy quietly dipped the paddle into the water and glanced over his right shoulder at the mammoth inky shape of *Liberator* forty yards away, her sleek profile distorted by the oppressive mantle of darkness to lend her the aspect of a surfaced sea monster from the deepest depths laying in wait for unsuspecting victims. He shook his head to dispel the imaginative comparison and faced forward, studying the shore they were slowly nearing.

A warm breeze blowing from the northwest mildly stirred the comma of hair that hung above Percy's right eye. Without moonlight to provide even feeble illumination the terrain was a blank black void hinting at latent menace.

The inflatable was only ten feet from land when Percy spied a flat strip of shoreline to their immediate right and promptly angled the boat toward the spot. He raised the paddle and motioned for Burroughs to do the same, letting their momentum carry them onto the beach. The instant the inflatable touched bottom he was up and over the side, the Franchi in his left hand. Using his right hand he pulled the boat from the sound and the seaman assisted him in hiding it in a stand of close-by trees.

Percy took his compass from a utility belt pocket and examined the illuminated needle and card, then hiked to the northwest. An eery silence shrouded the landscape. There were no lights anywhere. Not so much as a solitary lantern or light bulb indicated there was anyone else within miles of their location. He went twenty yards before he replaced the compass and raised the transceiver to his mouth. "Red Two to Red One."

"Red One here. Any problems?"

"None. It's as dead as the grave," Percy said, and wished he hadn't.

"Okay. We're going to dive and head out. Take care of yourselves. We'll be in transceiver range for the next ten minutes. If you need us, I'll turn the ship around."

"We'll be fine," Percy said, tempted to cross his fingers.

"Then we'll see you in thirty-five hours. Red One out."

Percy turned toward the sound and heard the familiar loud hissing as *Liberator* released the air in her main ballast tanks and took in water in preparation for diving. He listened until the sounds faded and he knew the sub was gone. Squaring his shoulders he tapped Burroughs on the arm and led the way inland.

The eeriness intensified the farther they went. Ordinarily wildlife noises would fill the night: the buzzing and chirping of insects, the croaking of frogs, perhaps the screech of a cat and the barking of dogs in the distance. But now there was nothing. Total, unnerving silence blanketed the countryside.

Percy felt as if he'd been shot into space and landed on an alien planet. He suppressed an uneasy sensation and concentrated on the mission. Proceeding cautiously he entered a tract of woodland that went on for a quarter of a mile. The trees abruptly ended and he took a couple of strides before he realized gravel was underfoot and they'd stumbled on an unpaved road running north and south. He opted for north, deciding to follow it to the first town.

The soft scuffing of their soles was the only sound. They traveled a half mile, then a mile. Up ahead abruptly loomed the silhouette of a two-story white frame house.

Halting, Percy studied the darkened windows and detected no sign of occupants. He gripped the Franchi firmly and advanced until he came to a chain-link fence. Should he check inside the house? No. There wasn't time to search every building they found. Besides, they needed a vehicle and there damn sure wasn't one in there.

Burroughs stood on his right, waiting patiently.

"We go on," Percy whispered, and did so. A fluttering arose at one of the upper windows and he attributed it to curtains rustled by the wind.

Soon the gravel road ended at a paved road. They took a fork that went to the northwest and hiked a few hundred yards before rounding a curve and discovering a small community before them.

Percy stuck to the center of the road. He wanted a clear field of fire if someone—or something—came at them. There were two vehicles parked on the right-hand side of the road, a battered pickup and a small car. He made toward them.

Suddenly, from behind one of the decrepit homes, came a metallic crash.

The short hairs on Percy's neck tingled as he stopped and spun. His heart tried to imitate a nuclear reactor and his blood pumped faster than a race car at the Indy 500. No other sounds shattered the stillness.

"An animal, you figure, sir?" Burroughs asked after a minute, his voice barely audible.

"Must have been," Percy responded in the same manner. He hurried to the pickup and frowned when he saw two of its tires were flat. The small car had a smashed windshield but otherwise seemed functional until he popped the hood and noticed the battery was missing.

They resumed their search, leaving the ghostly community behind, and went almost a mile before an isolated residence appeared on a hill to the west, its distinctive contours easily recognizable against the backdrop of sparkling stars. A driveway wound up to the home.

"Think it's worth a try, sir?" Burroughs wondered.

"Yes," Percy said, encouraged by the immense size of the house. Only a wealthy person or family could have afforded to live there, and rich types typically owned two or three vehicles. It was worth checking out. "On the double."

Side by side they jogged to the top of the hill. The driveway widened near a three-car garage attached to the rear of the residence. All the garage doors were closed, the parking area empty.

"Damn," Percy muttered, scrutinizing the gloomy windows. Nothing moved within. "Keep me covered," he directed, and stepped to the garage door nearest the house. Lifting carefully to minimize the noise, he raised the door to shoulder height and peered inside. Off to the left he detected the faint glint of metal.

"Sir!" Burroughs said.

Spinning, Percy saw the seaman point at the second floor. He swung around but spotted no one. "What did you see?"

"I'm not sure. I thought I saw someone staring out at us from the third window on the right. The face is gone now."

Percy waited for the person to reappear. Was it possible there were survivors in there? "Let me know if you see it again," he said. Stepping to the third door he quickly hauled on the handle, not concerned with stealth since whoever lived in the house was aware of their presence. He grinned in delight when the open door revealed an antique automobile in apparent perfect condition. The red exterior had been polished to a mirror finish. "Wow," was all he could think of to say.

Walking to the driver's door, Percy leaned in the open window and inhaled the musty scent of leather and wax. The owner must have restored the car to its original state. The bucket seats in the front were immaculate. He tried to recall the make and model without success. Eagerly he climbed in and gripped the steering wheel. If only he could start it! He checked the ignition, then under the seat, and finally ran his fingers on top of the sun visor. A whoop of excitement almost burst from his lips when he found the key held fast by a plastic clip.

Anxious to discover if the vehicle would serve their needs, Percy slid the key into the slot and twisted. Instantly the engine roared to thunderous life and the entire can shook. "Son of a bitch," he blurted, and leaned forward to examine the dashboard. He flicked on the lights and caught Burroughs in their glare.

The crewman squinted and screened his eyes with his left hand.

Percy glanced at the fuel gauge and chuckled. Nearly full. He felt like a kid in a toy shop at Christmas. Looking down between the seats he studied the stick shift. The car had a manual transmission. No problem. He'd driven Jeeps with manuals many times before.

"Mr. Percy!" Burroughs shouted, jabbing a finger in the direction of the house.

Not about to get out of the car for anything short of the end of the world, Percy tramped on the clutch, shifted from neutral into first, and tapped the gas pedal. To his astonishment the vehicle shot from the garage and almost ran over Burroughs, who madly darted out of the way a second before being bowled over. Percy slammed on the brakes and glanced to the left, his breath catching in his throat at the sight of three scarecrow figures dressed all in white shuffling swiftly toward him, their arms extended, their fingers rigid claws. "Get in!" he bellowed.

Burroughs yanked the passenger door open and jumped inside. "Go, sir! Go!"

For a moment Percy lingered, riveted by the horrific faces of the ghastly trio: their pale complexions marred by black dots that denoted festering sores, the red slits marking their mouths, and their wide, crazed eyes. He imagined he could feel their dilated pupils boring into his own.

The white-shirts were only a few yards off.

"For the love of God, sir! Get the hell out of here!" Burroughs yelled.

One of the things hissed.

Percy buried the accelerator, burning rubber, and the car rocketed forward. He looked in the side mirror and saw the white-shirts stop, and then he was zooming down the drive, shifting with surprising smoothness. "I think I'm in love," he commented to himself.

"Sir?" Burroughs asked, gazing out the rear window.

"Argyle, here we come."

17

"Contact ten miles off the port bow," Communications Officer Jennings announced.

Donovan swung the swivel chair around. They were out of Saint Andrew Sound and cruising northward in the Atlantic Ocean at flank speed. He now had added incentive to reach New York City as rapidly as practical and disliked being distracted. Come hell or high water he was going to make his rendezvous with Percy. "Put it on visual."

The surface ship materialized as a tiny colored stick figure, less than an inch in length, on the screen.

"We're getting more readings, Skipper, and they're all negative," Jennings said. "No engines, no sonar, and no heat generation whatsoever. A dead one, I think. Likely a small fishing vessel."

"Then we ignore it and stay on course."

Helmsman Hooper cleared his throat. "The ship is level at four hundred feet and making sixty knots. All systems are showing nominal. Automation is up and ready, sir. Should I engage?"

Donovan glanced at Jennings. "Any word from Mr. Percy?"

"No."

"Then engage automation, Mr. Hooper."

"Aye, Captain."

Donovan started to stretch when the tantalizing aroma of freshly brewed coffee tickled his nostrils. He glanced over his right shoulder to find Alex bearing a steaming mug. His mug.

"I thought you could use some refreshment," she said. "I know how you get at times like this. You forget to eat, to sleep, to change your socks."

"Are you implying my feet smell?" Donovan asked as he gratefully took the mug.

"No worse than a dead skunk lying at the side of the road."

Hooper uttered a sound that remarkably resembled the snort of a bull elk during mating season.

"Do you realize if you keep this up none of my men are going to take me seriously anymore?" Donovan asked with a grin.

"Don't worry on that score. They'll always treat you with respect."

"Oh?"

"You're a natural-born leader and they know it. Why do you think they voted to stick together under your command even though the U.S. Navy no longer exists?"

"They had nothing else to do."

"Pessimist."

Donovan took a sip and savored the delicious flavor as the coffee rolled over his tongue. "Did you make this yourself?"

Alex nodded. "I know we're low but I figured it might boost our spirits a bit. There are two pots waiting in the galley."

"Mr. Jennings, send four men at a time to the galley for ten-minute coffee breaks."

"My pleasure, sir."

Bending toward Alex so only she could hear, Donovan smiled and said, "I never expected you to make coffee for the entire crew."

"Why?"

"Somehow it seems too domestic for a liberated lady

like yourself," Donovan responded. He sipped another mouthful.

"That's what happens to a woman when she gets in the family way," Alex stated.

Astonishment stiffened Donovan's spine and made him sputter his coffee over the front of his shirt. "The family way?" he blurted, turning heads on the bridge.

"Not yet, but it could happen any day, you know. And I've been thinking about the likelihood a lot recently. What do we do then?"

"We cross that bridge when we come to it."

"Chicken."

"I'm serious."

"So am I, Tom."

"Now is hardly the proper time to discuss it."

"Fair enough. But don't take too long to decide when we should."

"Why?"

"Because I'm two weeks late."

"There are four more," Burroughs said.

Percy glanced to the right and spied the white-garbed quartet twenty yards from Highway 84. "I see them," he replied, frowning. Like the two dozen or so white-shirts they'd previously seen, these four were hurrying toward the highway at a walking run, which seemed to be the top speed they could attain. There was only one logical explanation: the things had heard the car and were trying to intercept it, indicating that the white-shirts were capable of associating the sound of an automobile with survivors and proving that the demented ghouls were capable of rudimentary thought.

"I get queasy every time I see one of those damn things," Burroughs commented.

"You and me both."

"What would they do with us if they caught us, sir?"

"They're not going to get their putrid paws on us."

"But what if they did?"

"Then they'd probably burn us to death, the same as they do with every living thing they catch."

"But why?"

"I wish I knew," Percy said, and glanced down at the map spread open on the seaman's lap. "Where are we now?"

Burroughs flicked on the thin black flashlight he'd taken from a pocket earlier and examined the map for the tenth time since they'd obtained the car. "We should pass a small town on the right called Hoboken any second."

"Hopefully it'll be like those other two we passed, Nahunta and Atkinson," Percy said. "Empty and peaceful."

"Isn't it strange that most of the white-shirts we've seen have been roaming the countryside instead of being in the towns?"

"Maybe not so strange. The white-shirts have undoubtedly cleaned out the cities and towns already. Now they're out scouring the rural areas."

"The whole thing is too creepy for words. I would hate to have been a survivor stuck in a major metropolitan area right after the war."

"Yeah. As it turned out, we were the lucky ones."

"God was watching over us."

"God? Are you religious, Burroughs?"

"Yes, sir. My folks were devout churchgoers. I guess their faith rubbed off on me. How about you?"

"My parents never had time for church. I was in my teens before I ever seriously thought about whether God exists or not."

"What did you decide?"

"I could never make up my mind. On good days I'd think there was a God, on bad days I'd swear there wasn't." Percy gazed to the left at more white-shirts. "Right at this moment I'm convinced the universe is run by a crazed zucchini with a perverted sense of humor." He pressed on the gas and watched the needle climb from sixty-five to seventy. The car left the white-shirts in the dust.

A sign informed them they were almost to Hoboken.

Percy stared straight ahead as he took a gradual curve, the tires squealing in protest, and then the car was on a straightaway and hurtling at a mob of white-shirts walking down the middle of the road toward it.

"Look out!" Burroughs cried.

The zombies broke into frenzied, lurching gaits, spreading out, trying to form a chain across the highway.

There wasn't time to slow down even if Percy had wanted to brake. He spun the wheel to the left, thinking he might be able to shoot around the things, but one of the white-shirts darted directly into the car's path. The sickening thud as the grille smashed into the man was nothing compared to what came next: the white-shirt exploded like a water balloon, the torso splitting in half and the head and arms flying in different directions. Pulpy flesh and grisly gore spattered onto the windshield and over the hood.

Percy almost lost control. The car went a dozen yards slewing from side to side until he gripped the wheel securely and brought the wheels back on the road.

Burroughs had his right hand over his mouth and was making gagging noises.

"Are you going to puke?" Percy asked, ready to stop if necessary. Already the white-shirts were a hundred yards to the rear and the reassuring rumble of the engine guaranteed he could easily elude them.

"No," Burroughs said, breathing raggedly. "I'll be okay." He lowered his hand and leaned back, spittle rimming his lower lip. "That was enough to make anyone toss their cookies."

"Some of the white-shirts do that when they're struck," Percy noted. "Donovan punched one in the face back in San Francisco and wound up with gunk all over his hand."

"Yuck."

Buildings came into sight on the right, deserted structures dark and foreboding like the landscape in general.

"Hoboken," Burroughs said.

The headlights played over the turf bordering the highway, revealing a charred mound of tree limbs and busted furniture that had once been a bonfire. Piled high on top were blackened skeletal remains.

"The white-shirts' dirty work," Percy stated harshly.

On into the night they raced. Burroughs consulted the map again. "Next up is a big town called Waycross."

"The one we can bypass to the south."

"Yes, sir. Highway 84 loops right around it. Then we have a twenty-two mile run to Argyle with just a dinky place called Manor in between."

They fell silent, each anxiously scanning the fields, forest and swampy areas bordering the road.

Percy saw an abandoned car on the left shoulder and was tempted to stop and check it out. They'd passed twenty or more so far, which had given him the germ of an idea on how to get the survivors in Argyle to Saint Andrew Sound. Provided, of course, they could devise a way to break out of the ring of white-shirts.

"Think this works?" Burroughs wondered, leaning forward to tap the radio. He reached for the knob, twisted until it clicked, and muted static hissed from the speaker.

"You won't pick up anything," Percy predicted.

Burroughs nodded but ran the tuning dial from one end to the other and back again anyway. On the return sweep he froze in astonishment when a faint voice proved them wrong.

". . . be off the air until eighteen hundred tomorrow on this same frequency. All citizens are advised to listen in for updates and instructions. Until then this is Site R signing off."

Static replaced the announcer.

Percy and the crewman exchanged startled glances. "That sounded like a government broadcast," he declared.

"What's Site R?"

"The name rings a bell," Percy said, striving to recall where he'd seen or heard the term before. Elation coursed through him and he beamed happily. Somehow, some way, the U.S. government had survived! America was down but not out!

"Do you think they received the broadcast on *Liberator*?"

"I hope so, but they might not have. We barely heard it, and if Donovan is sticking to his plan then the ship is sixty to eighty miles up the coast by now and four hundred feet down. We'll give a listen tomorrow at eighteen hundred and hope we get it again."

"What do we do if it is the government?" Burroughs asked.

"How do you mean?"

"Isn't it our duty to try and contact them? What then? Aren't we required to take orders from whoever is in charge? What if they want us to leave Espiritu and come back to the U.S.?"

"You ask too many questions," Percy said, troubled by the potential ramifications. Burroughs had a point. And although by all rights he should be overjoyed at the prospect of *Liberator* being mustered back into full-time military service, the possibility troubled him. "Besides, until we get more information there's not much we can do. For all we know, it wasn't a government broadcast."

The headlights unexpectedly revealed an animal crossing the highway.

"Look! A deer!" Burroughs exclaimed.

"A buck," Percy added, spying the rack of antlers crowning its head. He grinned, amused at how excited they were to sight so common a creature. Correction, he mentally noted. Once deer had been common; now they were as rare as normal human beings. Both were endangered species.

"What's it doing?" Burroughs asked.

The buck had stopped at the right-hand edge of the road and swung toward the car, which was sixty feet away and swiftly diminishing the distance.

"Maybe the lights have confused it," Percy speculated.

Suddenly the buck lowered its antlers and charged.

"That thing is crazy," Burroughs declared.

Crazed *and* dangerous, Percy reflected, because collisions with full-grown deer had often crushed the front ends of the vehicles involved, and they couldn't afford to let that happen to theirs. He kept the gas pedal down and tensed, ready to swerve aside at the last instant.

"What are you doing, sir?"

Percy didn't bother to answer. He focused on the buck to the exclusion of all else, and when the animal was only twenty feet in front of them he frantically rotated the steering wheel and sent the car veering to the left, onto the shoulder, then went to bring it back onto the highway while looking back to see the buck still charging off down the road.

A moment later the driver's side of the car seemed to sink down half a foot and the vehicle lurched to a growling halt, its tires spinning furiously.

"What the hell!" Percy snapped, letting up on the accelerator. He opened his door and leaned out to discover that both the front and the back tires were partly buried in muddy, swampy earth. "We've got a problem," he said.

"It's worse than you think," Burroughs stated.

"What?" Percy asked, straightening and gazing in the same direction as the crewman, at the field across the highway where a dozen or more white-shirts were hurrying toward them.

"Some of those things are carrying clubs or baseball bats," Burroughs said anxiously.

"Damn," Percy fumed, slamming his door. He threw the car into reverse and buried the gas pedal. The tires spun in a frenzy of centrifugal inertia, spewing dirt rearward, and the car rocked slightly but was held fast.

"They're about twenty yards away, sir," Burroughs noted.

Ignore them, Percy told himself, and shifted into drive again. He tramped on the accelerator and produced the same effect as before, only the car rocked harder and moved a few inches. In desperation he repeated the procedure again and again, first putting the transmission in reverse, then drive. Reverse, then drive. Each time the car moved a fraction more one way or the other.

"Ten yards," Burroughs reported, hefting his Franchi.

The roaring of the engine and the shrieking of the tires were all that mattered to Percy. Come on, baby, he wanted to say, you can do it! A few more inches and they would be out. Once more he threw the gearshift into reverse, and this time the car almost rose out of the ruts imprisoning it.

"Five yards."

Percy slammed the shift into drive and glanced to the right at the pale, demonic masks of death seemingly floating out of the darkness, closing on the car. He jammed the gas pedal to the floor, popped the clutch, and held on tight as the vehicle shook violently, swaying from side to side, and suddenly burst free, rocketing from zero to sixty miles an hour in seconds.

A heavy object struck the trunk as they pulled out, and then they were in the clear.

"We did it!" Burroughs cried.

Intent on angling back onto the highway, Percy simply nodded. Once the white-shirts faded into obscurity in the rearview mirror he bent forward and kissed the steering wheel.

Burroughs laughed. "You weren't kidding. You really are in love."

"Too bad I can't take this buggy back to Espiritu," Percy joked.

The narrow escape made them both subdued until they were almost to Manor. They said little and constantly scanned both sides of the road but saw no more white-shirts.

"Where did they all go?" Burroughs finally commented.

"Probably to Argyle. That guy we spoke to, Brick Wilson, claimed the survivors there are surrounded by hundreds. Every zombie for miles around must have converged on the town."

"Then the things must be able to communicate."

"But how?" Percy wondered. "We've heard white-shirts grunt and roar and bellow, but no one has reported hearing a white-shirt talk. They apparently lose the power of speech when the transformation takes effect." He paused, bothered by a possible oversight. "Or maybe we've simply assumed they did."

Buildings appeared ahead, another small town.

"This is Manor," Burroughs said. "Only seven more miles to Argyle, sir."

"I bet those folks will be overjoyed to see us," Percy predicted. He envisioned how delighted the colonists on Espiritu would be when *Liberator* returned with the

Southerners. The island could accommodate hundreds more survivors and still maintain an adequate ecological balance.

"I've been meaning to ask you, sir," Burroughs said, interrupting the executive officer's introspection. "What kind of car is this? I'm not an expert on these antiques."

"Neither am I," Percy admitted, looking at the dash. "I don't know what kind it is."

The crewman opened the glove compartment. "Hey, look at these." He pulled out a stack of papers, placed them on top of the map, and held the flashlight up so he could read them. "The registration is made out to a Barry Winsett. Says here this car is a Chevrolet Chevelle. And talk about ancient. You'll never guess the year this model came out."

"1980?"

"1968." Burroughs crammed the papers back into the glove compartment. "My grandfather might have driven a car like this."

"How old are you, Burroughs?"

"Twenty-one, sir."

Percy frowned. Why do I suddenly feel old? he asked himself. I'm only thirty. He tilted his neck to relieve a slight cramp and scoured the highway ahead for signs of Argyle. "I'll have to kill the lights when we're close to town," he forewarned the seaman.

"Understood," Burroughs said.

They drove for several minutes without incident.

"What in the world are those?" Burroughs abruptly asked, doing a double take.

Percy saw them at the same instant, a half dozen bright mounds of flame over a mile to the southwest, at the exact spot where Argyle should be.

"Are they campfires?"

"No. They're too big," Percy answered, and the implication staggered him.

"Bonfires," Burroughs breathed in horror.

"Please, no," Percy said, and applied the brakes while switching off the lights. He let the car come to a complete stop before rolling down his window to listen. Clearly on the cool night air wafted a wavering scream.

"Dear God," Burroughs declared.

"We'll get as close as we dare, then go the rest of the way on foot," Percy said, bringing the speed up to thirty miles an hour.

Both of them sat tensely on the edge of their seats. The crewman rolled down his window, amplifying the second scream when it came moments later.

After traveling half a mile Percy reduced the speed to twenty miles an hour and drove cautiously down the center of the road. Soon homes cropped up on both sides and the metallic throbbing of the engine echoed eerily. Abandoned cars were parked along the curbs.

"We've gone far enough," Percy said, and pulled into a driveway on the right. He reluctantly killed the engine. The sudden heavy silence hung about them with an indefinable air of palpable evil.

"Why am I shivering?" Burroughs whispered. "It's not cold."

Percy felt a slight quivering in his own limbs that galvanized him into action to ward off the fear. "Let's go," he said, and climbed out. Closing the door quietly, he heard the shriek of a man float by on the brisk breeze.

"God help us," Burroughs said, shutting the passenger door. He inadvertently jumped when the latch clicked.

"Get a grip, seaman," Percy chided him.

"Sorry, sir."

"Stay close," Percy directed, and hiked in the direction of the bonfires. He double-checked the Franchi's selector lever to be sure he had the weapon set on full automatic, then touched each grenade, reassured by the physical contact. We can handle the white-shirts, he told himself. Stay calm.

Off to the right a twig snapped loudly.

Percy promptly dropped to one knee and Burroughs imitated his example. They waited a minute but there were no other sounds.

Motioning with his left arm, Percy rose and continued toward the blazing mounds. There were six in all, and countless figures, distinct in their white apparel, were moving about nearby. The bonfires had been constructed in two rows of three mounds each outside a high stone wall bordering a house.

As Percy drew closer using every available cover, he distinguished additional details. A gate in the middle of the wall had been thrown wide and white-shirts were coming and going, carting furniture and other flammables to be used for fuel from within and then heading back for more. Scores of the zombies were gathered around the fires to watch the burning. A large delivery truck had been backed up against the wall on the east side, next to piled stacks of crates, trash cans, tires, and various other items. Standing on top of the truck were eight or nine zombies.

Not until Percy came to a lilac bush twenty yards from the crowd of vile abominations and peeked around it did he see the burning corpses piled on the top of each mound. He bowed his head in sorrow, shocked to his core. They were too late! The white-shirts had breached the wall and overrun the survivors.

"Sir! Look!"

Percy glanced up and saw a group of seven white-shirts hauling a male survivor toward a bonfire, only this man was alive; he appeared to be injured but was resisting the crazies with all his might, jerking and twisting in a frenzied effort to break free.

"We've got to help him," Burroughs said.

"We wouldn't stand a chance," Percy replied, appalled at his own callousness. But self-preservation dictated they shouldn't intervene. There were at least eighty or ninety white-shirts viewing the burnings and many more on the grounds of the house.

The man resisted even harder the nearer he drew to the flames. "Get your filthy hands off me!" he bellowed. But neither his desperate thrashing nor his words had any effect.

Inexorably, moving like wooden automatons, the white-shirts forced their struggling captive to the edge of a bonfire. He screamed as they bodily lifted him overhead, and his scream became a strident, soul-wrenching shriek when they took a few strides in unison and heaved him into the fire.

The man landed hard on his side and instantly tried to scramble to his feet. But the flames were so high, the blistering heat so intense, that his clothes were engulfed before he could rise halfway. A plaintive wail issued from his lips as he managed a halting step, then pitched backward, his arms and legs swinging wildly.

Burroughs turned away, unable to endure the sight.

"We did our best to get here," Percy said. "This isn't our fault."

"Do we head back?" the crewman asked hopefully.

"What else can we do?"

More white-shirts appeared, coming through the gate with two survivors clasped in their clammy hands, two defiant prisoners who were fighting as best they were able even though their size and age rendered their resistance futile. They were children, a young boy and girl.

Percy took a step and blurted, "No!"

"Sweet Jesus," Burroughs exclaimed. "We can't let them die."

For a second Percy hesitated, his reason telling him any rescue attempt would certainly result in his death, that the odds were hopeless, that only a fool threw away his life when there was no hope of survival. But then the girl cried out and he charged around the lilac bush into the full harsh glare of the bonfires, impelled by something deep within him, a feeling he couldn't reason away. His heart went out to them and he grit his teeth in a grim determination to rescue the children or die in the attempt.

All the white-shirts were observing the progress of the party bearing the boy and girl to their awful deaths. Many of the crazies were clustered in large groups loosely connected by thin lines of demented onlookers.

Percy made for a weak point in the ring encircling the fires, where nine or ten white-shirts were strung out over a fifteen-yard stretch. He barely noticed that the inhuman killing machines wore a variety of clothes; shirts, T-shirts, sweaters, jackets, and whatever else they had found that was white or close to it. Some of them wore clothes that had been spray-painted their mysterious color of preference. Every garment was streaked with grime and spattered with mud and blood.

The line of crazies Percy bore down on had their backs to him. None of the white-shirts had yet awakened to his presence. He had the element of surprise in his favor and he intended to take full advantage of it. His right hand closed on an M40 white phosphorous "acid grenade," a grenade that had been developed at the turn of the century and could spew out great clouds of acidic smoke for up to a minute. The chemical agent wasn't lethal but it would burn the eyes and sear the lungs of anyone who inhaled it. Using a fragmentation grenade was out of the question; there was too great a risk of the children being hit by a fragment.

Twenty feet separated the girl and boy from the crackling flames.

Percy halted, yanked the pin, and hurled the acid grenade into a crowd on the right. Swiftly he grabbed a second one and threw the gray, spherical canister into another group on the left. Both began to disgorge their contents on impact, enveloping the nearby white-shirts in a grimy cloud.

Leveling the Franchi, Percy sprinted forward and squeezed off a short burst, whipping the barrel in a tight arc. The rounds bored into the line of crazies barring his path, their backs rupturing as the slugs smacked home. He downed half a dozen, and then he was through the gap and racing toward the kids.

Belatedly the assembled zombies not immersed in acid clouds reacted to the attack. A few started toward him.

Percy ignored them. He also ignored the tremendous heat that made him break out in large beads of sweat and caused his face to feel as if he were simmering over a red-hot grill.

Two of the six white-shirts holding the children let them go and turned toward him.

He shot high, elevating the barrel enough so that his next rounds punctured heads instead of torsos. The pair dropped, and then he was close enough to the remaining four to see the sores on their skin and the flat, malevolent hatred in their eyes.

Both children seemed astounded by his advent. The boy, a dark-haired kid of ten or eleven, recovered first and renewed his attempt to tear himself free. His slightly older sister did the same a moment later.

Percy had to wait until he was only a few yards from the bonfire detail before he could fire again, not wanting to hit the boy or girl by mistake. He raised the Franchi to his shoulder, aimed carefully, and sent slugs into the heads of the last four white-shirts in the party.

The zombies were thrown backwards by the impact, their fingers torn loose from the children, and crashed to the earth.

"Come on!" Percy shouted, motioning for the kids to follow, and whirled to retrace his route.

Already the assembled crazies were closing ranks and converging on them.

19

Percy paused to extract the partly spent magazine in the Franchi and tossed it aside. He pulled a fresh one from a utility belt pocket, his fingers flying, his eyes roving in all directions, and slapped it home. The gap he had blasted in the ring of white-shirts was gone, filled by other ghastly specters. Looking over his shoulder he found the boy and girl right behind him, gazing up at him in relieved wonder. We're not out of the woods yet, he wanted to say, and instead started toward the line of zombies.

Somehow news of the rescue attempt had spread among the white-shirts on the grounds of the survivors' stronghold and more were pouring through the gate.

For several heart-pounding seconds panic seized Percy and he nearly lost control, nearly cut loose wildly and sacrificed himself and the children on the altar of primal instinct. He focused his thoughts, angling toward the exact spot where he initially broke through the crazies, and took aim.

Another Franchi chattered mercilessly and a dozen of the white-shirts fell, some convulsing violently, saving Percy the trouble. Seaman Burroughs had entered the fray, dashing into the open and providing covering fire. He shouted, "Hurry, sir! I'll keep them back!"

Percy didn't dare run at his full speed for fear of outdistancing the children. He jogged rapidly in Burroughs's direction, constantly checking to ensure that the kids were keeping up. A pack of white-shirts came too close on the right and he discouraged them with a dozen rounds. The biggest threat came to his left, where the zombies rushing from the gate formed a compact mass of rabid killers.

Spinning this way and that, firing selectively, Burroughs was successfully mowing down white-shirts to keep a path open.

"Keep going!" Percy directed the boy and girl, and motioned for them to hurry past him. Rotating to the left, he swallowed hard, beholding the wave of demented creatures cresting toward him. A fragmentation grenade fit snugly into the palm of his right hand as he snatched it off a utility belt and extracted the pin using his teeth. Just like the Duke, he reflected, his favorite actor of all time, and he marveled that he could entertain so ridiculous a thought with his life on the line. Taking two swift steps he hurled the grenade in a high loop, then spun and raced after the children.

The ball-shaped pineapple came down well behind the front ranks of white-shirts and the Composition D explosive, the standard explosive used in U.S. grenades after 2001, exploded, hurling fragments of the metal body in all directions. Every crazy within twenty yards was caught in the blast. Those nearest the impact point were shredded; those farther away sustained grave wounds.

For a few precious seconds the white-shirts halted, looking about blankly for the source of the explosion.

The children reached Burroughs and he waved them on, holding his ground until Percy came alongside him. "Keep going, sir. I'll cover you."

Nodding, Percy caught up with the girl and boy and stayed abreast of them as they ran past the lilac bush. A glance back confirmed the white-shirts in mass pursuit. Soon Argyle would be crawling with them.

Burroughs was back-pedaling, firing as he did, mowing more down.

"We have a car but it's a ways off," Percy told the kids, his voice sounding unnaturally strained. "Can you hold up?"

"Yes, sir," the boy answered on the run.

"I'll try," the girl responded.

"What are your names?"

"Randy."

"Janet."

"Stick close to me. With luck we'll get out of this mess alive," Percy said, and led their flight through the muggy Georgia darkness. They covered a hundred yards. Ahead, to the right, a bunch of white-shirts materialized, hastening toward the bonfires.

The things promptly changed their course to intercept the fleeing humans.

Percy pressed the Franchi to his side and fired, holding the barrel as steady as he could, and killed half of them before the submachine gun went empty. He grabbed for a new magazine.

"Allow me, sir," Burroughs said, coming up from behind the kids to add his firepower to the fray. In moments the grass was littered with twitching corpses.

They continued on in silence. Percy twisted to see a virtual army in pursuit and a slight shudder rippled down his spine. Thank goodness most of the white-shirts were too emaciated to possess much endurance. Most, but not all.

A score of the fleetest were well out in front of their fellows and showed no sign of tiring soon.

Can we reach the car ahead of them? Percy asked himself, dreading the consequences if they didn't. He looked at the children, admiring the fierce determination on their faces, wondering what horrors they'd witnessed during the final battle. Should he inquire about their parents? No, he decided. Not until they were safely away from Argyle.

Percy gazed back at the bonfires and the high walls. Were there other survivors still alive in there? Had they heard the gunfire and gotten their hopes up? He hoped not. He prayed not.

Over halfway to the car another small band of white-shirts popped into view to the north. They were hastening toward the fires and failed to notice the four humans.

The girl began to breathe raggedly, her steps faltering. "I don't know if I can go any farther," she said weakly.

Slowing, Percy lifted her in his left arm, surprised at how heavy she was, seventy or eighty pounds, at least.

Randy glanced at his sister, his mouth set in a tight line, but his own legs were betraying his willpower.

Without being told, Burroughs stepped in close and clasped the boy in his left arm.

"I can manage," Randy protested.

"Take a break anyway," Burroughs said. "Besides, I can use the exercise."

For the next couple of minutes all went well. They came within a hundred yards of their Chevy and were jogging down the middle of a side street when the pounding of heavy footsteps to their rear emphasized the perilous reality that they were far from out of danger.

Percy glanced over his shoulder and discovered a trio of white-shirts, the swiftest of the zombies, only a dozen yards off and rapidly closing the gap. "Burroughs!" he shouted, halting to deposit Janet on the ground.

The foremost white-shirts carried, of all things, a machete. He raised the long blade on high for a killing stroke.

Training the Franchi on the crazy's chest, Percy squeezed the trigger in the expectation of cutting the man to ribbons. Instead, he heard a loud click as the submachine gun jammed. There was no time to make the weapon work and he couldn't move aside and expose

Janet to the thing's attack. His right hand streaked to the Colt on his hip, and in a blur of motion his arm swept up and out.

The white-shirt was only a yard away and starting his downswing.

Percy fired, the .45 blasting and bucking in his hand. The bullet slammed into the man's forehead and hurled him rearward, causing the other two to swing wide to avoid being bowled over.

Seaman Burroughs took out the pair with a short burst.

"Look out!" Randy suddenly cried, pointing to the right.

Rotating, Percy's breath caught in his throat. There were a dozen crazies thirty feet distant. Where the hell had they come from? "Take the kids and go!" he ordered, slinging the Franchi over his left shoulder and drawing his other Colt.

"We're not leaving you," the crewman said, and took several strides. He dropped to one knee, aimed, and sent a swarm of 9-mm hornets buzzing into the pack of bloodthirsty killers. Two-thirds were slain in the blink of an eye, but the rest advanced undeterred.

"I'm empty," Burroughs cried, snatching a fresh magazine from his utility belt.

Now it was Percy's turn to move in front of his companion, extend both Colts, and fire nonstop, one pistol after the other, *BAM-BAM-BAM*, the heavy recoil of the big .45s jerking his hands upward after each shot. The many hours he'd spent on the firing range paid off. He might not be in Charlie Donovan's class, but he was no slouch in the firearms department, either.

The slugs took the white-shirts down one by one, each struck squarely in the center of the chest, a few striving to rise even after they were down.

"Reloaded," Burroughs said.

Percy holstered the Colts and unslung the Franchi. He worked the bolt until a round fed properly into the chamber. "Let's get the hell out of here," he prompted, scouring the landscape for more white-shirts. There were none, but the shots were bound to draw more. Lifting Janet, he hastened to the car and breathed a sigh of relief when he finally stood beside it.

"White-shirts!" Burroughs exclaimed, nodding to the southwest, where a large band was in hot pursuit.

The children were quickly placed in the back seat. Percy slid behind the wheel, inserted the key, and twisted.

Nothing happened.

Both men exchanged glances and Percy tried again.

A low growl sounded under the hood but the engine refused to turn over.

"The battery, you think?" Burroughs asked.

"I don't know. I'm not a mechanic," Percy said, staring at the band that was only fifty feet off. He turned the key and held it down. The growling went on and on, growing progressively feebler.

"What's going on?" Randy wanted to know.

"*Please* get us going," Janet added.

Crossing the fingers on his left hand, Percy twisted the key once more. The growl became a roar as the engine thundered to life. Instantly he shifted into first, switched on the headlights, and got out of there, resisting an urge to flip a finger at the white-shirts because of the kids. The car sped down the highway, leaving the zombies far behind. He let his body relax.

"We did it," Burroughs stated happily.

"We did nothing," Percy corrected him, and looked at the children. "What are your last names?"

"Lamb, sir," Janet said.

"Both of you? You're brother and sister?"

"Yes, sir."

"There's no need to call me sir," Percy informed her.

"Are you a general or something?" Randy asked.

"I'm the executive officer on a submarine. My name is John Percy. You can call me John."

"Yes, sir," Randy said.

Percy indicated the seaman. "And this is Tom Burroughs."

"Call me Tom."

The children studied the men, their features evincing slight apprehension.

"What are you planning to do with us?" Janet inquired.

Percy roved his eyes over the road and the land on both sides. Now was as good a time as any to ask them the million-dollar questions, he decided, and hoped they wouldn't become too upset. "Before we get to that there are a few things I must know. First, where are your parents?"

Janet sadly bowed her head.

Randy clenched his fists and declared, "They're dead. Those freaks killed them."

"Can you tell us about it?" Percy probed.

"It was a couple of months ago," Randy detailed. "We were hunting for food in a town south of here, going through the stores looking for cans of peaches and beans and such, when a pack of those things jumped us in an alley."

"The white-shirts?"

"Is that what they're called? My dad called them freaks and my mom said they were the walking dead."

"What happened?" Percy asked.

Randy's voice lowered drastically when next he spoke. "We were trapped. The dead ones had the way out blocked off. Our dad and mom got us to the back of the alley and lifted us on their shoulders so we could climb into a window in this big building. Then they told us to run." He fell silent and gazed out the window.

"There's no need to finish," Percy said, wanting to spare them the nightmare of going into detail. "But tell me. How did you get to Argyle?"

"We lived like animals for a long time, sneaking around and getting what food we could, and then met up with a man named Meyers and his little girl Nadine," Randy related. "He brought us here looking for friends of his. When we got to town there were no freaks, just a bunch of nice people. Some of them got here in a bus a while back and stayed when the bus broke down."

"They were really nice," Janet emphasized. "Everything was okay until those things showed up. At first there were just a few and the men killed every one of them. Then more and more came until one night a whole army poured into the town and all the people went to Mr. Ferguson's place for protection."

Percy had heard enough. He could imagine the rest. There was no need to upset them more than they already were. "How would you like to live at a place where there are no white-shirts?"

"Is there such a place?" Janet asked.

"Yes, on an island in the South Pacific. The submarine that dropped us off on the coast will be back to pick us up and take us there. If you want to join us you can come live on the island. A lot of families call it home and I'm sure one would be happy to take you in."

"Are there kids like us?" Randy queried in disbelief.

"Quite a few, actually. You'd have plenty of friends to play with. It's sunny there all year long and you can swim in the ocean whenever you want."

"Sounds like heaven," Janet said.

"The island is called Espiritu."

Randy leaned forward. "Would we have to go to school?"

"I'm afraid so. The parents were in the process of organizing one when we left."

The boy looked at his sister and frowned. "I knew it sounded too good to be true."

"Anything, Mr. Jennings?" Donovan asked.

The communications officer shook his head. "The airwaves are dead, Captain. I've tried all civilian bands and priority military channels."

"What about ASCS?" Donovan inquired, referring to the Atlantic Submarine Communications Satellite high in a parked orbit at 23,500 miles above the earth.

"We burst-transmitted to ASCS and got no response, just like with the PSCS bird."

"Is the ASCS still up there?"

"Affirmative, Skipper. It relayed our message to every ground station in the U.S.," Jennings reported, and frowned. "Zilch."

Donovan leaned back in his chair and idly stared at the screen, then checked his watch. Seven A.M. They were making good time. Only nine hours had elapsed since dropping off his X.O. and they were already due east of Washington, D.C. Initially he'd allotted thirteen hours to reach the vicinity of New York City, but now it appeared they would get there in eleven, possibly twelve. Not bad at all. He'd told Percy to expect the ship back in thirty-five hours, giving himself a comfortable nine-hour safety margin on the round trip in case of problems. If everything continued to go smoothly they would be back at Saint Andrew Sound well ahead of schedule.

Of course, if they made contact with other survivors then the timetable would be thrown off. (Which was the reason for the safety margin.) But the prospect of locating others became slimmer with each passing hour. All along the East Coast the situation had been the same. None of the major cities had exhibited a hint of life; there were no transmissions whatsoever. Savannah had been as dead as the proverbial doornail. Charleston, the same. Norfolk, Portsmouth, Richmond, and now Washington, D.C., were all electronic graveyards.

An idea occurred to Donovan and he looked at Jennings. "What about Mount Weather?"

Located in Virginia, Mount Weather was one of approximately fifty top-secret command-and-control centers scattered throughout the country. It was one of the biggest, an enormous underground facility capable of housing one thousand people and stocked with enough supplies to last for several years. U.S. contingency plans had called for the nation's political leaders and top military brass to be flown there at the outset of any nuclear war. As with other such sites Mount Weather was supposedly able to withstand everything but a precise hit.

"Nothing from there," Jennings replied. "I've been trying other bunkers, too, without success."

"Strange," Donovan said. "You'd think there would be a few bunkers intact. Neither the Germans nor the Soviets knew the location of all of them. Hell, they were kept secret from everyone except those with a need to know."

"For that matter," Jennings commented, "I'm surprised we never heard a peep out of Kneecap."

Donovan nodded thoughtfully. Kneecap was the nickname for NEACP, which in turn stood for the National Emergency Airborne Command Post, a special Boeing 747 crammed with state-of-the-art telecommunications gear. There had been four such Kneecaps and one had always been kept in the air. A second was always fueled and waiting at Andrews Air Force Base, only ten minutes from the Capitol by helicopter. Surely there had been time for some top officials to get aboard and take off.

"What's Kneecap?" Alex asked, coming up to the chair. She'd just walked onto the bridge and overheard the comment.

It took but a minute for Donovan to explain.

"Perhaps the jets were caught in firestorms," Alex speculated. "We know the firestorms were extensive over the U.S., but we don't know how high into the atmosphere they reached. Any air traffic caught in one wouldn't last two minutes."

"Your explanation would also account for not hearing a peep out of Looking Glass," Donovan mentioned.

"What does *Alice in Wonderland* have to do with World War Three?" Alex cracked.

"Looking Glass was the code name for four aircraft based at Offutt Air Force Base in Omaha, Nebraska. If war broke out, SAC planned to use them as airborne command posts."

"Kneecaps. Looking Glass. I would have loved to meet the guy responsible for inventing code words."

"How do you know it was a guy?"

"Because the hierarchy of the military-industrial complex was a bastion for men. Females were rarely elevated to top ranks or performed highly classified jobs, so I'd say the odds are that men prepared the codes."

"I think your bias is showing again."

"Oh, yeah? Then tell me something, smart guy. How many women submarine commanders were there in the U.S. fleet?"

"None," Donovan admitted.

"I rest my case."

"You missed your calling," Donovan told her with a grin. "Instead of being a scientist, you should have become a lawyer."

Alex smiled. "If I had, I undoubtedly wouldn't be standing here right now razzing the hell out of you."

Jennings suddenly interrupted their banter. "Captain, Sensors reports multiple targets twelve miles ahead off the port bow."

"Put them on the screen."

"Aye, sir."

Eight icons promptly materialized clustered together, their configurations clearly military.

"Is it a task force?" Donovan wondered in disbelief.

"Negative," Jennings replied. "We're getting sonar registry. There's a destroyer, the U.S.S. *Raymond*. We've also got a radar picket escort vessel, two minesweepers, two repair ships, a transport vessel, and, believe it or not, a tug."

"Mainly support ships," Donovan noted.

"There are no energy readings, no temperature differentials. They're dead, just floating with the current."

"So what else is new?" Donovan said bitterly. Once, just once, he'd like to find another naval vessel intact and its crew alive. He studied the icons. "It must have been a convoy of auxiliary ships heading out to sea when they were caught in the fringes of a blast or a firestorm."

"Those lousy firestorms again," Jennings commented.

"How's the air up there?"

"The atmosphere is clean. Normal radiation readings."

Alex spoke up. "Which is to be expected after so many months. All the atmospheric particles have long since been dispersed by the winds or settled down to earth."

Helmsman Hooper surprised everyone by chiming in. "Captain, can I ask a question?"

"Certainly."

"There's something I've been curious about. Do you remember all that talk about a nuclear war causing a nuclear winter?"

"Yeah."

"Why didn't it?"

Donovan glanced at Alex. "You want to handle this one?"

"Gladly. There are two reasons we're not experiencing a nuclear winter. First, many of the missiles employed were of the neutron or FAE variety, which don't produce that much radiation, and most of the thermonuclear devices that were used were set off as air bursts instead of ground bursts," Alex explained.

"What's the second reason?" Hooper inquired.

"Nuclear winter was a concept advanced by an astronomer who claimed the smoke from nuclear blasts would blot out nearly all sunlight. The media picked up on his statements and sensationalized them, like they did everything else."

"And his claims weren't true?"

"No. He should have stuck to gazing through a telescope. Later scientists at the National Center for Atmospheric Research conducted an extensive study using a three-dimensional computer that was one of the forerunners of our Cyclops. The results of their study conclusively repudiated the nuclear winter scenario," Alex detailed. "Certain people and groups with political motivations kept the idea alive, but among scientific circles it was entirely discredited."

"I didn't know," Hooper said.

Alex frowned. "It's always been the same. A crazy idea becomes popularly accepted and all the scientific evidence in the world won't change the perception of those who want to believe it."

"Like what?"

"Take the acid rain fiasco back in the eighties and nineties. People got all worked up over our lakes supposedly becoming pools of lethal acid, but that just wasn't the case. Congress authorized a ten-year study in 1980 to the tune of five hundred million dollars. Called the National Acid Precipitation Assessment Project, it involved seven hundred of the top atmospheric, soil, aquatic, and agricultural scientists in the nation. They found no evidence whatsoever that acid rain was a real threat. So what did Congress do? They forked out a hundred and forty billion to clean up lakes that didn't need cleaning," Alex concluded.

Donovan looked at her and chuckled. "You're amazing, do you know that?"

"How so?"

"You're like a walking encyclopedia."

Alex grinned. "I knew all along that you love me for my mind."

"Vanquished again," Donovan said, and decided to get back to the matter at hand. He swung his chair forward. "Mr. Hooper, take us up. Since we're ahead of schedule we'll take the scenic route."

"Yes, sir."

"Mr. Jennings, I want a warrant officer and a gunnery detail ready to go topside the moment we break the surface. And just to play it safe we'll mount a Walther."

"What can harm us out here?" Alex asked idly.

"You never know."

Picture perfect was the only way to describe their surroundings: an azure sky dotted with floating white islands wafted on a slow breeze; a calm sea rippled by tiny waves, stretching into infinity to the east and breaking on the shore a mile to the west; and gulls squawking overhead while denizens of the ocean occasionally leaped out of the water in graceful arcs.

"You'd never know there has been a war," Alex commented as she surveyed the beautiful setting.

"Ain't it the truth," Donovan said. He was surveying the coastline of Delaware through binoculars. Nothing moved, not a boat or ship in the bays and inlets or any vehicles on land.

Alex gazed up at the dozen or so seabirds soaring above *Liberator*. "At least the gulls aren't attacking us like those we ran into in the Pacific."

"Don't give them any ideas," Donovan cautioned, lowering the binoculars. "Mr. Hooper, increase speed to thirty knots and take us in closer. A quarter mile out should suffice."

"Thirty it is, Captain," the helmsman responded from his topside post. "And a quarter mile."

Donovan moved aft and glanced down at the crew manning the Walther to shout, "Hang on tight, gentlemen."

Soon they were abreast of Delaware Bay. Once oceangoing vessels had regularly plied its waters to take the Delaware River beyond, traveling inland one hundred miles to Philadelphia, the largest freshwater port in the world. Now there wasn't a vessel in sight.

Staring at the placid bay, Donovan was tempted to alter course and proceed into the Intercoastal Waterway, as the Delaware system had once been known. Philadelphia had served as the headquarters for the Fifth Naval District and boasted a huge naval shipyard. If the City of Brotherly Love hadn't sustained a hit there might be naval units there. A *big* if. He realized he was indulging in wishful thinking and kept on course.

The coast of New Jersey, once bustling with a flourishing tourist trade, lay quiet and deserted. The famed Atlantic City boardwalk was still intact but the only living creatures strolling along in the sunshine were birds.

Alex held a pair of binoculars she was using to intently scan the shore. "It's as if someone decided to wipe the slate clean and start all over again," she commented.

"Strange we haven't seen many white-shirts," Donovan said.

"Aren't they more active at night?"

"Yes, but there's usually some abroad during the day."

"Perhaps they're finally starting to die off. We knew it was only a matter of time before the toxins in their systems wiped them out."

"We've hoped that was the case," Donovan corrected her.

Atlantic City, the East Coast's answer to Las Vegas, stood stark against the skyline, the casinos resembling enormous tombstones. Not one of the city's fabled neon lights were lit. Past the gambling mecca lay a series of islands, none displaying a trace of habitation.

The intercom blared to life and Jennings reported, "Captain, there's a small target lying dead in the water nine miles off the starboard bow."

"Thanks. Keep me posted," Donovan responded.

Minutes later Donovan spotted a small yacht. His pulse quickened when he saw someone seated on the foredeck, and he quickly brought his binoculars to bear.

"Is it—?" Alex asked excitedly, doing the same.

"No," Donovan told her grimly.

A partly rotted corpse sat tilted backwards, braced by the slanted cabin trunk. It wore only jeans. An insane smile exposed its upper and lower teeth. The eyes were gone, their sunken sockets dark pits. Scattered all around the body on the foredeck were dozens of beer cans, most empty and crushed.

"Partied to the last," Alex said softly.

"I can't wait until we're back at Espiritu," Donovan mentioned.

Suddenly the intercom crackled again and Jennings made an electrifying announcement. "Skipper, radar has picked up an aircraft approaching, bearing one-nine-zero."

"An aircraft!" Alex exclaimed.

Donovan swung to the southwest and scoured the sky as the communications officer elaborated.

"Range is fifteen miles. Altitude only five hundred feet. Speed is one hundred and ninety-two miles per hour." Jennings paused. "It's definitely making straight for us." He paused once more. "Computer enhancement of profile characteristics shows it's a chopper."

A helicopter? Going that fast? Donovan couldn't see it yet. He stepped to the intercom and stabbed the button. "Have you established radio contact?"

"Trying, sir. But they won't answer."

"Keep trying. Warn them off. Tell them if they come too close we'll be forced to fire."

"Aye, Captain."

Alex glanced at him. "What's wrong? Why fire?"

"How do we know a crazy isn't piloting the 'copter?" Donovan responded, raising his binoculars. "Right after the war we were buzzed by a Russian in a MIG-15 who kept trying to strafe us even though he had no ammo. In Seattle there was that guy in the Boston Whaler who attacked us. In Tahiti there was the native in a piroque."

The implications etched worry lines in Alex's face. "For a second there I got my hopes up."

Donovan moved to the aft rail and yelled down to the gun crew. "Incoming aircraft bearing one-nine-zero. Be ready to fire at my command."

"Yes, sir," came the prompt reply.

The men rotated the Walther in the appropriate direction.

"There it is!" Alex declared.

Spinning, Donovan looked and spied a small dot on the horizon that rapidly grew in size. He couldn't believe the thing's speed. One second the chopper was miles away, the next less than a mile off and abruptly decelerating. Now he could distinguish details, and what he saw only mystified him further.

The helicopter was black: black fuselage, black stabilizer, black rotor blades, and twin black engines. Even the cockpit had been tinted black to screen those within from scrutiny. Its contours were sleek, its appearance futuristic in the extreme. Resembling an enormous dragonfly, the chopper halted a thousand yards from *Liberator* and hovered.

"I don't see any markings," Alex remarked.

Donovan didn't either. Its presence sparked a hundred questions. Who were they? What did they want? Why wouldn't they respond? Although no armaments were visible, he believed it was a military craft. He realized the copter wasn't making any noise; the spinning rotor blades were completely silent.

"What kind of helicopter is that?" Alex asked.

"I don't know," Donovan admitted, and used the intercom again. "Mr. Jennings, any answer yet?"

"Negative, Captain."

Donovan glanced at the 'copter and came to a decision. "Lasers on. Probe mode. Prepare to fire on my order."

"Yes, sir."

Liberator's lasers were the outgrowth of technology initially devoted to surface-to-sub communications. Fired from turrets fore and aft of the blister, the lasers could be used either as weapons or as data-gathering probes. In the weapons mode the system had an effective range of

1,000 yards; in the probe mode the range was extended to 10,000 yards.

Shifting, Donovan looked at Hooper. "Helmsman, all stop."

"All stop it is, Captain."

Liberator slowed, the spray over her bow diminishing as she cut back from thirty knots to zero.

The mystery 'copter started to come closer, flying slowly.

"Lasers activated, Skipper," Jennings reported. "Sensors reports a good lock on the target."

"I want all probe information recorded for later analysis," Donovan said.

"Of course, sir," Jennings responded, sounding a bit miffed at being reminded of such a standard procedure. "The Cray-9 peripheral input module is on-line. CPU has acknowledged control code."

"Then fire."

"Commencing fire."

Twin bursts of blue-green light shot from the turrets, striking the helicopter in the cockpit. Almost instantly the craft banked and swooped off in a tight loop. The lasers were still locked on, the computer automatically tracking the target, and the narrow beams raked the chopper from its nose landing light to its tail rotor. Then the 'copter dramatically increased speed and sped off to the southwest, dwindling to the size of a flyspeck in less than ten seconds.

"Lasers off," Donovan ordered.

"Deactivating lasers, sir."

The two blue-green lights blinked out.

Helmsman Hooper was grinning ear to ear. "That showed 'em, Captain. Maybe the next time they'll see fit to answer us."

"If they don't fire a missile or something," Alex spoke up, looking at Donovan. "You must have spent hours watching those old westerns on the tube when you were a kid."

"I did, as a matter of fact. How did you know?"

"It shows. You're always ready to shoot first and ask questions later."

"Do you blame me?"

Alex stared at the now-empty sky to the southwest. "No, not under the circumstances. Not at all."

Moving closer to the rail, Donovan thoughtfully surveyed the coastline. "Whoever they are, they must have a base of operations within a few hundred miles of here at the most."

"Why?"

"Because a helicopter like that must use a lot of fuel. I doubt that it has a very extended range," Donovan said.

"I have the feeling we haven't seen the last of it," Alex stated.

"Maybe so, but we're not sitting here waiting for it to come back. Mr. Hooper, bring us to twenty-five knots."

"Yes, sir."

Alex laughed lightly in relief. "I guess we've had our little excitement for the day."

"There's bound to be more," Donovan said.

As if in confirmation, over the intercom came Jennings's urgent voice. "Captain to Communications. We're picking up Espiritu."

Donovan adjusted the headset and eagerly gripped the microphone. "Charlie, can you hear me?"

"Just barely, big brother," was the faint reply.

"The same here," Donovan said.

"What's going on there? We've been trying to raise you without success. Is your equipment malfunctioning?"

"Our equipment is fine. We've been trying to contact you, too. Atmospheric interference is the problem. It's been ten times worse since the war. Over."

"Tell me about it. How is everything else?"

"Fine. We're almost to New York. How about at your end? Have you identified the man-eaters yet?"

"Yeah. It's a pack of wild dogs. Over."

"Dogs? Did I hear you correctly? Did you say *dogs*?" Donovan asked, and listened attentively while Charlie related in detail recent events on the island. As his brother concluded, the transmission began to break up. "I'm having trouble hearing you. Do you copy?"

Only static hissed in the headphones.

"Pirate, do you copy?"

There was no response.

Jennings studied a dial on his console. "Did you lose him, Captain?"

"Yes," Donovan said. "Try getting him back."

The communications officer spent the next five minutes diligently attempting to reestablish contact. At length he looked at Donovan and shook his head. "Sorry. I'll keep trying but it might take a while. Frankly, I'm surprised we received them at all at this time of day. Reception is always better after sunset."

"Let me know if you get lucky."

"Did we hear you correctly?" Alex asked. "Have they found dogs on Espiritu?"

"A pack of wild ones," Donovan confirmed.

"That accounts for the howling," Alex said, pondering. "And it's the only explanation that makes complete sense."

"How do you figure?"

"European seamen explored the Pacific Ocean extensively a few hundred years ago. On many islands they left behind dogs, hogs, and rats, which usually resulted in ecological disaster. One prime example was the dodo, a big bird that lived on an island in the Indian Ocean and was completely wiped out by the imported species."

"So you think seafarers left some dogs on Espiritu and the animals survived all this time?"

"That'd be my guess. There's plenty of game and water on the island," Alex noted.

"But what about the natives? Why didn't they domesticate the dogs or, failing that, wipe them out?"

"Who knows? The dogs might have hid out and had nothing to do with the natives. Even if the islanders tried to tame them, it's extremely hard to domesticate animals that have fully reverted to their wild state," Alex speculated. "And since Espiritu is a big island it would have been easy for the dogs to elude hunters."

"Let's hope Charlie can find their lair before more people are killed," Donovan said, removing the headset.

"Has anyone else been attacked since we sailed off?"

"No," Donovan replied. "But they do have another mystery on their hands."

"Such as?"

Donovan told her about the enormous mound of bones.

"I don't know what to make of it," Alex said when he concluded. "I'll reserve judgment until I see the bones for myself."

"Which hopefully will be quite soon," Donovan said. He placed the headset on the console and glanced at Jennings. "The crew will want to know we've heard from home. Put a message on every monitor on the ship."

"What should it say?"

"Something short and sweet," Donovan said, then went on, "Everyone on Espiritu alive and well and sends their regards. Man-eaters found to be dogs. Precautions have been taken and situation under control. Will update after next contact. The Captain."

Jennings began typing on his keyboard. "Right away, sir."

"We'll be topside if you need us," Donovan stated, and led Alex up the ladder into the bright sunlight. Hooper was handling the helm. A warrant officer had binoculars trained on the shore.

"A lot of gulls off the port side aft, Captain," the young helmsman reported.

A glance confirmed the presence of hundreds of raucously squawking sea gulls a hundred yards from *Liberator*, flying from east to west.

"They don't appear interested in us," Donovan said.

"Thank God," Alex declared, recalling the time they were attacked and severely pecked.

"Captain, take a look at this," the warrant officer said, sounding shocked.

Quickly Donovan stepped over and took the binoculars. At first he saw only a sandy beach, a strip of highway beyond bordered by a string of telephone poles, and then a row of frame houses. "I don't—" he began, then tensed, spying the bodies hanging *from* the poles, over a dozen in all, dangling from the crossbeams. There were men, women, and children.

Alex got a hold of another pair of binoculars and looked for herself. An intake of breath signified she'd seen the corpses.

"This is a new twist," Donovan said somberly.

"Do you think the white-shirts were responsible? I thought they burned all survivors."

"Apparently they don't burn everyone they capture. In Dutch Harbor in the Aleutians we found bodies hung on meat hooks," Donovan said. He detected movement between two homes and felt a chill ripple down his spine when a group of crazies came into view attired in their typical white clothing. Seven, he counted.

"Tom," Alex said.

"I see them."

The white-shirts moved woodenly into one of the houses.

"What are they doing?" Alex wondered.

"Who the hell knows," Donovan growled. He watched for over a minute as the sub sailed northward, but the pack of killers didn't reappear.

"It's unfortunate *Liberator* doesn't have an isolation chamber," Alex mentioned. "We could capture a white-shirt and study it, maybe finally isolate the specific cause of their condition."

Donovan looked at her. "What would it take to construct such a chamber?"

"Are you serious?"

"I'm ready to try anything. Waiting around for those things to die off could take a lot longer than any of us have figured. We either need to find a way to cure them or a means of wiping them out."

"I'll talk to Pete. He'll know better than I what materials and equipment we'd need."

"Get back to me with a list."

"Yes, sir," Alex said, and grinned impishly.

"Captain?" Helmsman Hooper interjected.

"What is it?"

Hooper pointed. "New York City dead ahead."

New York City. Once a teeming metropolis throbbing with the pulse of life. Once the leading city in the world, the cultural hub of the United States, a center for global shipping, for financial institutions, industrial activities, and political machinations. The city had everything: Broadway, Radio City Music Hall, the United Nations headquarters, the American Museum of Natural History, Central Park, and so much more. A forest of skyscrapers towered to the heavens. Millions of tourists from all over the globe traveled there to see this ultimate monument to human accomplishment.

What a difference Armageddon had made.

Absent were the bustling millions, the streams of cars and trucks, the swirl of nonstop activity. Absent were the skyscrapers and every other building for miles around. Absent was every vestige of a superior civilization.

New York City was in ruins.

None of the five boroughs that had occupied the land at the mouth of the Hudson River still existed. Charred, twisted spires were all that remained of the grand skyscrapers that once dominated vivacious Manhattan. Mounds of blistered wreckage and piles of blackened debris littered the landscape, forming a gloomy labyrinth. The devastation was total.

Liberator neared the Lower Bay at a cautious clip of twenty knots. Donovan intently scanned the shore, studying the twin wastelands of Staten Island and Brooklyn situated on either side of the Narrows. Memories of his parents and their apartment on Riverside Drive tugged at his heartstrings. At least, he consoled himself, they must have died instantly, incinerated in the fiery heat of the nuclear explosion.

"How awful," Alex commented sadly, lowering her binoculars, appalled by the destruction.

Donovan nodded and pressed the intercom button. "Environmental report, Mr. Jennings."

"I was just about to buzz you, Captain. If we stay away from the city proper we'll be okay. Sensors indicate ambient radiation readings off the scale over the length and breadth of the blast radius. Obviously a ground strike."

"Atmospheric readings?"

"Marginal. There's no need for radiation-protection suits unless we get within a few hundred yards of the hot zone."

"I suppose it's ridiculous to ask, but is there any electronic activity?"

"None, Skipper."

"Okay," Donovan said. "Send the following message on all frequencies. Perhaps someone farther inland will hear and respond." He paused, composing the wording. "U.S.S. *Liberator* to all survivors. Kindly reply immediately."

"Is that it?"

"Yeah. Short and sweet. Program the transmitters to broadcast the message every five minutes until we leave."

"Will do."

"Anything at all from Ronca and Hardesty?"

"Not a peep."

"Damn. Keep me posted." He straightened and gazed to the northeast, recalling the directions Sal Ronca had provided. "Mr. Hooper, what about channel reflectors, buoys and the like?"

"There are none, sir."

"Figures. And we can't take advantage of the Cray's topographic features file because New York City doesn't have any features left to speak of. Very well. We wing it," Donovan said, and trained his binoculars in the direction of Ambrose Channel.

"There's plenty of clearance under the keel, Captain," Hooper mentioned. "No obstructions to speak of yet."

"Take us in toward Rockaway Point. Slow to fifteen knots."

"Yes, sir."

Liberator's teal-colored hull barely broke the surface as she crept closer to the shoreline. It soon became apparent the nuclear blast had done in seconds what would have taken erosion a million years to perform: Lower Bay was now more like a gulf. Much of Brooklyn and the eastern third of Staten Island were under water. The thin finger of land once comprising Rockaway Beach, Rockaway Park, and Rockaway Point had also been inundated. Scattered islands existed where once had been Manhattan Beach, Coney Island, and Sheepshead Bay.

Donovan contacted Communications again. "Mr. Jennings, what can you tell me about those islands off the bow?"

"Some are hot, some are not."

"You missed your calling. You should have been a poet."

A metallic chuckle issued from the speaker, then Jennings elaborated. "None are as hot as the mainland. Those farthest out are the safest."

Helmsman Hooper suddenly spoke up. "Captain, there's a lot of submerged debris around those islands. Keel clearance looks iffy."

"Take us to within a quarter mile of the outermost island, then all stop."

"Aye, Captain."

"Mr. Jennings, I want a small arms detail topside pronto. I also want an inflatable and three volunteers to accompany me."

"On their way."

Alex came closer, nervously chewing on her lower lip. "I trust you're going to wear suits?"

"No," Donovan replied. "They're bulky and awkward. If we run into white-shirts we can't afford to have our movements restricted."

"But the radiation," she objected.

"I know the landmarks on the island we're looking for. Since Ronca and Hardesty have survived there all this time, the radiation must be minimal."

"You hope."

Soon the small arms detail and the crewmen bearing the inflatable bustled onto the deck. Three seamen armed with Franchis came up, ready to go with their captain.

Shortly thereafter Helmsman Hooper reached the designated distance from the shore and declared, "All stop, Captain."

Donovan turned to Alex and their eyes met and lingered in a mutual expression of their deep affection. After a bit he cleared his throat and said, "See you soon." Pivoting, he climbed from the topside bridge to the deck.

"Take care of yourself," Alex called down.

Small waves lapped at *Liberator*. A warm breeze from the northwest caressed her streamlined contours. Overhead were a few gulls, circling and squawking.

Taking a deep breath, Donovan strode briskly over to the waiting crewmen. The inflatable was already in the water and ready to go.

"Here you are, sir," said one of the men, who handed over a gunbelt containing a pistol, a Franchi and six spare magazines, a transceiver and an EnviroTester.

Donovan geared up, giving the EnviroTester to one of the volunteers. He climbed into the boat without another word, waited until his three men were seated, and gave the order to shove off. Staring straight ahead, he beheld the sinister expanse of murky water dotted with small, potentially lethal islands and suppressed a budding shudder.

"Captain, look," one of the crewmen said, pointing to the west.

Complying, Donovan spied a column of gray smoke curling up into the sky. Was it a white-shirt bonfire or a cooking fire started by a survivor? Probably the former; no survivor in his or her right mind would be abroad in the region with so many crazies roaming about. He activated the transceiver. "Mr. Jennings, do you copy?"

"Five-by, Skipper."

"Sensors pick up anything yet?"

"Not a thing, sir."

"Just checking. Keep the channel open in case."

"Will do."

Donovan clipped the transceiver to his belt and picked up the EnviroTester. Adjusting the controls took a few seconds. As Jennings had reported, there was no danger of radiation contamination from the atmosphere. He checked the water and saw the needle move just a fraction. It was truly amazing, he reflected, how readily Nature bounced back from humanity's ongoing onslaught on the ecological balance. He recalled reading about Hiroshima and Nagasaki and how fifty years after the dropping of the bombs both cities were flourishing, filled not only with throngs of people but boasting countless beautiful gardens and tracts of healthy trees. It gave him hope that planet Earth would one day recover from this last folly.

The volunteers paddled quickly, efficiently, in concert as they'd been trained, bringing the inflatable ever nearer the outlying islands.

Donovan studied those closest. Some were little more than barren mounds. Others had shattered buildings on them or were piled high with debris. A few, amazingly, bore shrubs and thin, anemic trees.

"Where are these folks we're looking for, sir?" asked one of his men.

Sal Ronca's words echoed in Donovan's mind: "We're holed up in the clock tower of the old college building. You can't miss us. We got the only windmill in this part of town." He glanced at his men. "On an island with a clock tower and a windmill."

"Then it shouldn't be too hard to find, Captain."

It wasn't. Two minutes later an island materialized bearing the unmistakable silhouette of both landmarks. Excited, they paddled rapidly and went around its west end.

Donovan was about to use binoculars when he heard a slight hissing noise to his left and shifted to discover a large shark fin knifing the surface twenty feet off. He reached for his Franchi, then changed his mind. The shark was going from north to south, passing them by. Why invite trouble by trying to kill it? He focused on the island instead.

Something moved, stepping from the clock tower where a shattered door hung by one hinge, and shuffled toward the water.

A ripple ran down Donovan's spine and his breath caught in his throat. A white-shirt! A rotten white-shirt! He swept the binoculars right and left, finding more zombies, fifteen or twenty at least. No! No! No! His teeth gnashed as he scoured for any sign of Ronca and Hardesty, rage filling him, rage at himself for not leaving

Espiritu sooner, for letting down two families when they needed help the most.

The inflatable drew closer. All three crewmen clearly saw the zombies.

"What are we going to do, sir?" one asked.

Donovan wondered the same thing. Logic told him both families had been wiped out. But if so, where were the bodies? Nor was there any evidence of a bonfire. He scanned the narrow beach and saw a row of twenty or more logs or telephone poles and large, flat sections of wood including an intact door. The significance eluded him until moments later when the crazy that had emerged from the tower shoved one of the logs into the bay, slowly eased down on top of it, and mechanically paddled with its arms, making for the distant shore.

A rush of horrifying insight enabled Donovan to imagine the sequence of events: The white-shirts had organized a crude flotilla and managed to reach the island, perhaps drawn by any light visible from the city. Most likely the zombies made the journey at night when Ronca and Hardesty and their families were asleep. He envisioned the things creeping up on the unsuspecting survivors and scowled.

Another shark fin appeared, heading straight for the paddling white-shirt. The predator narrowed the gap swiftly and seemed certain of attacking, but at the last second it inexplicably veered away.

"Did you see that?" one of the men declared in amazement.

"What do you make of it, Captain?"

"I'm not sure," Donovan said. "Maybe the shark wasn't all that hungry." Somehow, he doubted it. He made a mental note to ask Alex and Peter later.

The men were still paddling and the inflatable was

only thirty yards from the island.

"Are we going to land, sir?"

"Yes," Donovan stated, lifting the Franchi. "We have to be sure the survivors are dead. Double-check your weapons, gentlemen."

Several of the zombies spied the approaching men and moved toward the shore.

Donovan knelt and tucked the Franchi's stock against his ribs. He trained the submachine gun on the leading white-shirts, who reached the water's edge, halted, and clawed the air expectantly. Despite his revulsion and a strong temptation to cut loose, he forced himself to wait, to hold off until the inflatable was only ten feet from them, and then he squeezed the trigger and held it down, the Franchi blasting and recoiling as he swept the barrel from right to left.

The slugs bored into the crazies' chests, dotting their torsos with holes, and five of the sore-infested automatons dropped soundlessly.

More were hurrying toward the bay now, aware of the humans and eager to reach them.

"Get set," Donovan bellowed, quickly removing the partially spent magazine and slapping home a new one. "Fan out and let the bastards have it."

Additional white-shirts were coming from the tower and the windmill to join their ghastly comrades.

Tensing his legs, Donovan vaulted over the side the instant the boat touched the ground. Zombies were only six feet away, and he crouched and sent a blistering swarm of lead into their heads and bodies, felling them on the spot, dreading the thought of even one of the things getting close enough to lay a hand on him.

The three crewmen cleared the inflatable. One pulled it higher while his buddies opened fire, slaying white-shirts right and left, carefully dividing the field of fire between them. The third seaman joined in, killing four crazies with a short burst.

Donovan's weapon went empty. He replaced the spent magazine, his fingers flying, watching six more white-shirts walk out of the clock tower. How many were in there? he wondered, and stitched all six with a swift sweep.

Above the din of the four Franchis rose a shriek of warning from one of the men. "Captain! Look out!"

Pivoting, Donovan's skin crawled at discovering a white-shirt on his right, less than a yard off, its baleful eyes alight with a feral eagerness to reach him, its arms stretched out, pus oozing from its many blisters. He frantically straightened and back-pedaled, firing madly, pouring half his magazine into the vile monstrosity, holes blossoming all over its face and upper chest, the impact propelling the thing rearward to crash onto the ground.

The three crewmen were spreading out in combat squad formation, slaying the white-shirts with superb efficiency.

Again Donovan reloaded, worked the cocking bolt, and slowly advanced, firing selectively.

Scores of white-garbed bodies dotted the tract between the water and the structures, many convulsing or twitching, their mouths working, their hands clenching and unclenching.

Skirting the corpses in his path, Donovan slew the last of the zombies still upright and paused as an eery silence descended. He glanced at his men, ensuring they were all right, then at the clock tower and the windmill. There were no more white-shirts.

"We did it!" one of the men cried.

Donovan stepped warily toward the tower entrance. "Stay out here and keep watch," he directed. "I'm going in."

"Shouldn't one of us go with you, sir?"

"I'll go alone. If you hear shooting, come running," Donovan said. He didn't bother to add that there wouldn't be a lot of room to maneuver in there and a lone man would have greater freedom of movement and be able to fire indiscriminately without the fear of accidentally hitting a mate. Stepping to the right of the doorway, he paused and listened.

The place was as quiet as a tomb. To the left of the tower stood the partly crumbled remains of a college building, clearly uninhabitable.

Donovan eased inside, his nerves primed, his fingers lightly touching the Franchi's trigger. A ten-foot-square room that must have served as the main living area for the Hardestys and the Roncas was now a shambles, the furniture busted, several lanterns lying broken on the floor. He saw no bloodstains or anything to indicate the occupants had been slain. Where the hell were they? Had the white-shirts somehow taken them off the island? Or were their corpses lying farther in?

He crossed the living area to a narrow corridor and discovered a stairwell. Should he go up or down? Darkness shrouded the levels below so he went up. On the next floor were rooms containing several beds, all of which had been flipped over and the sheets and blankets torn off. Still no survivors, though.

Donovan went up to the top of the tower, carefully inspecting each floor, finding only various belongings smashed by the white-shirts. Frustrated, he returned to the ground floor just as one of his men shouted.

"Captain, are you okay?"

"Fine," Donovan responded. Removing his lighter from his left pocket, he lit it and started down the stairs into the bowels of the building. The oppressive gloom gave him a spooky feeling. He swore he heard faint scratching sounds from behind the walls and wondered if rats were the cause.

On the next floor he found rooms that had contained boxes of provisions. Every box had been torn apart and its contents upended. There were cans of food, ammunition, medical supplies, and other items covering every square inch. He found a flashlight, flicked the switch, and discovered to his delight that it worked. Putting the lighter back in his pocket, he began to go down the next flight.

"What happened to the families?" he muttered, certain he was wasting his time, that his hunt would prove fruitless.

The next landing was the last. On all sides were buckled walls and mounds of dirt. Donovan played the flashlight beam over the rubble, his shoulders sagging. He'd failed. Failed miserably. He wanted to find a hole and crawl into it. The responsibility had been his and his alone. Delaying the ship's departure from Espiritu had been a terrible mistake, a misjudgment he would have to live with for the rest of his life. Anger flared and he vented his resentment of his stupidity by harshly declaring, "Damn me all to hell!"

"Who said that?"

Donovan whirled at the sound of the voice, sweeping the beam over a shoulder-high pile of dirt on his right. "Who's there?"

"I asked you first," a man responded.

"It can't be a crazy," chimed in a second man. "They don't speak."

Stunned, his pulse racing, Donovan moved nearer. Those voices sounded familiar. Not as tinny as on the shortwave, but the same. The pile, he found, had been deliberately placed a foot out from a portion of wall. And there, in the middle of the wall, was one of the sweetest sights he'd ever laid eyes on: a closed door. "Sal? Pete? Is that you?"

"Oh, my God! It's Donovan!"

Squeals of delight and whoops of joy arose on the far side of the door, and suddenly the handle was twisted and out poured two men, two women, and six kids.

Donovan stood stock-still as they swarmed happily around him, tears in most of their eyes, patting him on the back and shoulders and all of them talking at once in an ecstatic jumble of intense gratitude.

"I'm Sal," Ronca introduced himself. "This is my wife Marge."

"And I'm Pete," Hardesty declared, and indicated a brunette by his side. "This is Lorraine."

The men launched into introductions of their children, but Donovan barely heard them. Tears abruptly streamed down his cheeks and his temples pounded, not from pain, but from the sheerest joy he'd ever known, an elation so profound and so exalted it transcended any relief he'd ever felt. For a minute he didn't move, unable to even speak.

Gradually the families quieted.

"Donovan?" Pete said.

Nodding, Donovan coughed twice and said, "Sorry. It's great to find you alive. I thought—" He stopped, leaving the sentence unfinished.

"We would have been," Sal stated, "if we hadn't prepared this room as our last line of defense. Originally we intended to erect a fence around the island, but we couldn't find the materials."

"The crazies attacked in force two nights ago," Pete revealed. "We fought them as long as we could, then brought our families down when the things started to batter in the front door. Occasionally we'd hear them moving around out here. Thank God they didn't have the brains to think to look behind the dirt."

Donovan dabbed at his eyes and indicated the stairs. "I hate to cut this short, but we'd best get going. I'll radio for another inflatable to be sent and in no time we can have you safely on *Liberator*."

"Safe," Pete said, almost reverently. "You don't know how good that word sounds."

"I think I do," Donovan said, and they all laughed.

Epilogue

An hour later *Liberator* sailed southward at thirty knots bearing ten people whose happiness was contagious. The families went through the sub from bow to stern, meeting every member of the crew and personally thanking each one for their rescue. If any crewman had entertained lingering doubts about the captain's plan to venture anywhere and everywhere in search of survivors, those doubts were eliminated.

On the topside bridge stood two people who were almost as joyous. Donovan couldn't seem to stop smiling. He even forgot himself so far as to take Alex's hand and give it an affectionate squeeze. "This is what it's all about."

"You'll get no argument from me."

"Did you see the looks on their faces?"

Alex grinned at the look on *his* face. "I sure did."

"This trip has taught me a lesson. The next time we receive a plea for help, we head right out."

"I admire a man who's decisive."

Donovan glanced at her and lowered his voice. "If you weren't in the family way, I'd show you a little of that decisiveness tonight."

"Don't let that stop you," Alex said. "I won't break."

"We'll see," Donovan declared, a twinkle in his eyes. He inhaled and gazed at the blue sky. "I can't wait to pick up Percy and head home so I can break the news to Charlie."

"How do you think he'll take it?"

"He'll be jealous."

"Jealous?" Alex repeated.

"Yeah. He started riding me a few years back, teasing me that he'd end up having kids before me," Donovan related, and grinned. "Now I get to prove him wrong."

"Congratulations."

"Congratulate yourself. You'll be doing most of the work."

"True."

Donovan suddenly recoiled as if from a staggering thought. "Oh, no!"

"What is it?" Alex asked, concerned.

"Where the hell am I going to find pickles on Espiritu?"

They survived Armageddon to sail the oceans of a ravaged nightmare world

OMEGA SUB 76049-5/$2.95 US/$3.50 Can
On top secret maneuvers beneath the polar ice cap, the awesome nuclear submarine U.S.S. *Liberator* surfaces to find the Earth in flames. Civilization is no more—once-great cities have been reduced to smoky piles of radioactive ash. As their last mission, the brave men of the *Liberator* must seek out survivors in the war-blackened land.

OMEGA SUB #2: COMMAND DECISION
76206-4/$2.95 US/$3.50 Can

OMEGA SUB #3: CITY OF FEAR
76050-9/$2.95 US/$3.50 Can

OMEGA SUB #4: BLOOD TIDE
76321-4/$3.50 US/$4.25 Can

OMEGA SUB #5: DEATH DIVE
76492-X/$3.50 US/$4.25 Can

Buy these books at your local bookstore or use this coupon for ordering:

Mail to: Avon Books, Dept BP, Box 767, Rte 2, Dresden, TN 38225
Please send me the book(s) I have checked above.
☐ My check or money order—no cash or CODs please—for $ _____ is enclosed
(please add $1.00 to cover postage and handling for each book ordered to a maximum of three dollars—Canadian residents add 7% GST).
☐ Charge my VISA/MC Acct# _____ Exp Date _____
Phone No _____ I am ordering a minimum of two books (please add postage and handling charge of $2.00 plus 50 cents per title after the first two books to a maximum of six dollars—Canadian residents add 7% GST). For faster service, call 1-800-762-0779. Residents of Tennessee, please call 1-800-633-1607. Prices and numbers are subject to change without notice. Please allow six to eight weeks for delivery.

Name _____
Address _____
City _____ State/Zip _____

SUB 0192

CREATED TO SERVE, NOW THEY'RE DEDICATED TO DESTROY HUMANKIND

by Mark Grant

MUTANTS AMOK 76047-9/$2.95 US/$3.50 Can

They had been bred as the perfect killing machines—vicious, fearless warriors genetically designed to triumph on the battlefields of the 21st century. But the mutant servants have revolted and a small band of human rebels—their one-time masters—are the last hope of a besieged planet.

MUTANTS AMOK #2: MUTANT HELL
76048-7/$2.95 US/$3.50 Can

An attempted revolt by a brave but foolhardy band of *Homo sapiens* guerrillas has been crushed. Their captive leader, Max Turkel, is faced with a grim and terrible choice: either slow, agonizing death at the hands of his inhuman enemies... or collaboration.

MUTANTS AMOK #3: REBEL ATTACK
76191-2/$2.95 US/$3.50 Can

MUTANTS AMOK #4: HOLOCAUST HORROR
76192-0/$2.99 US/$3.50 Can

CHRISTMAS SLAUGHTER
76457-1/$3.50 US/$4.25 Can

Buy these books at your local bookstore or use this coupon for ordering:

Mail to: Avon Books, Dept BP, Box 767, Rte 2, Dresden, TN 38225
Please send me the book(s) I have checked above.
☐ My check or money order—no cash or CODs please—for $_____ is enclosed (please add $1.00 to cover postage and handling for each book ordered to a maximum of three dollars—Canadian residents add 7% GST).
☐ Charge my VISA/MC Acct# _____ Exp Date _____
Phone No _____ I am ordering a minimum of two books (please add postage and handling charge of $2.00 plus 50 cents per title after the first two books to a maximum of six dollars—Canadian residents add 7% GST). For faster service, call 1-800-762-0779. Residents of Tennessee, please call 1-800-633-1607. Prices and numbers are subject to change without notice. Please allow six to eight weeks for delivery.

Name _____
Address _____
City _____ State/Zip _____

#1

HIS THIRD CONSECUTIVE NUMBER ONE BESTSELLER!

James Clavell's
WHIRLWIND

70312-2/$6.99 US/$7.99 CAN

From the author of *Shōgun* and *Noble House*—
the newest epic in the magnificent Asian Saga
is now in paperback!

"WHIRLWIND IS A CLASSIC—FOR OUR TIME!"
Chicago Sun-Times

WHIRLWIND

is the gripping epic of a world-shattering upheaval that
alters the destiny of nations. Men and women barter for
their very lives. Lovers struggle against heartbreaking odds.
And an ancient land battles to survive as a new reign of
terror closes in...

Buy these books at your local bookstore or use this coupon for ordering:

Mail to: Avon Books, Dept BP, Box 767, Rte 2, Dresden, TN 38225
Please send me the book(s) I have checked above.
☐ My check or money order—no cash or CODs please—for $_____ is enclosed
(please add $1.00 to cover postage and handling for each book ordered to a maximum of
three dollars—Canadian residents add 7% GST).
☐ Charge my VISA/MC Acct#_____ Exp Date _____
Phone No _____ I am ordering a minimum of two books (please add
postage and handling charge of $2.00 plus 50 cents per title after the first two books to a
maximum of six dollars—Canadian residents add 7% GST). For faster service, call 1-800-
762-0779. Residents of Tennessee, please call 1-800-633-1607. Prices and numbers are
subject to change without notice. Please allow six to eight weeks for delivery.

Name _____
Address _____
City _____ State/Zip _____

JCW 0291

FROM PERSONAL JOURNALS TO BLACKLY HUMOROUS ACCOUNTS

VIETNAM

DISPATCHES, Michael Herr
01976-0/$4.50 US/$5.95 Can
"I believe it may be the best personal journal about war, any war, that any writer has ever accomplished."
—Robert Stone, *Chicago Tribune*

M, John Sack
69866-8/$3.95 US/$4.95 Can
"A gripping and honest account, compassionate and rich, colorful and blackly comic."
—*The New York Times*

ONE BUGLE, NO DRUMS, Charles Durden
69260-0/$4.95 US/$5.95 Can
"The funniest, ghastliest military scenes put to paper since Joseph Heller wrote *Catch-22*"
—*Newsweek*

AMERICAN BOYS, Steven Phillip Smith
67934-5/$4.50 US/$5.95 Can
"The best novel I've come across on the war in Vietnam"
—Norman Mailer

Buy these books at your local bookstore or use this coupon for ordering:

Mail to: Avon Books, Dept BP, Box 767, Rte 2, Dresden, TN 38225
Please send me the book(s) I have checked above.
☐ My check or money order—no cash or CODs please—for $_____ is enclosed (please add $1.00 to cover postage and handling for each book ordered to a maximum of three dollars—Canadian residents add 7% GST).
☐ Charge my VISA/MC Acct#_____Exp Date_____
Phone No _____ I am ordering a minimum of two books (please add postage and handling charge of $2.00 plus 50 cents per title after the first two books to a maximum of six dollars—Canadian residents add 7% GST). For faster service, call 1-800-762-0779. Residents of Tennessee, please call 1-800-633-1607. Prices and numbers are subject to change without notice. Please allow six to eight weeks for delivery.

Name_____
Address_____
City_____ State/Zip_____

NAM 0391